The Domino Image

B.J. Hoff

ACCENT BOOKS
Denver, Colorado

ACCENT BOOKS

A division of Accent Publications, Inc.
12100 West Sixth Avenue
P.O. Box 15337
Denver, Colorado 80215

Library of Congress Catalog Card Number 86-70648

ISBN 0-89636-218-3

For Mary Nelson—

A Christian—
And an Editor—
With the courage of her convictions

Philippians 1:3

AUTHOR'S NOTE:

My sincere thanks to
Cedar Point Marketing Department
Sandusky, Ohio
for questions so graciously answered and
information so generously supplied.

*"Crowds may praise
And nations cheer,
The whole world may applaud . . .
But above the noise,
His own will hear
The still, small voice of God . . . "*

B.J. Hoff
From *Voices*

Prologue

July

The man on the beach tugged at the zipper of his navy windbreaker, then shoved his hands deep into the pockets of his jeans. He stared for a moment more at the small, dollhouse-like cottage he'd been watching for over an hour, then turned and walked away.

She hadn't come out of the cottage tonight. Last night and the evening before, she'd gone walking. But not tonight. He could see a soft glow of light behind the drapes, and once the door had opened just enough to admit a small gray and white cat. But he hadn't caught even a glimpse of her before she disappeared behind the closed door.

He stopped walking and looked in the direction of the pier. His gaze fastened on the white lighthouse just beyond, its red light blinking through the thick, overcast dusk. The air off Lake Erie was damp and heavy, unusually cool for July.

After a few seconds he ran a hand through his hair, passed it over the back of his neck in a gesture of fatigue, then resumed his long-legged, uneven stride. He hurried down a narrow lane between two rows of inexpensive cottages, crossed an alley, and turned into a dark, isolated street. After unlocking the door of a dusty black sedan, he glanced around, then quickly slid behind the steering wheel, his head brushing the roof of the car. He punched the key into the ignition and immediately pressed the power door lock. His hands trembled slightly on the steering wheel as he waited for the engine to warm up.

He glanced at his watch, then pulled a small penlight from the glove compartment of the car. Focusing a stream of light on the seat beside him, he flipped through the pages of a black ring binder until he found what he wanted. He stared for a long time at a newspaper photo beneath a transparent sheet protector. Finally his gaze moved to the article beneath the picture. Lowering the penlight, he scanned the brief article, clipped from *The Nashville Banner* three years earlier.

. . . Vali Tremayne continues to be unavailable for comment regarding her career plans. The top female vocalist in the exploding contemporary Christian music industry for over two years now, Miss Tremayne is said to be recovering from an emotional collapse following the recent tragic death of her fiance, composer and vocalist Paul Alexander, in an airplane crash over the Appalachian Mountains.

Joanne Seldon, Miss Tremayne's agent, has also refused to discuss her client's future plans. Sources say, however, that Miss Tremayne has "retired" and is presently recuperating at a lakefront resort in northern Ohio. If this information is accurate, it could mean that Miss Tremayne has chosen to live near the family of Paul Alexander.

The deceased musician's mother, renowned novelist and literary award winner, Leda Alexander, resides in San-dusky, Ohio. His twin brother, Dr. Graham Alexander, is a well-known and highly respected research scientist who founded Alexander Center, one of the largest and most influential research centers in the country. The Center is located in northern Ohio, and Dr. Alexander makes his home in Port Clinton . . . .

The man in the black sedan looked up from the news article long enough to drop a cassette tape into the car player. For several moments, he sat unmoving, staring straight ahead, his fingers on the steering wheel drumming a mindless accompaniment to the rich female voice on the tape.

A few minutes later, he switched off the penlight, eased out of the parking place, and headed for the highway. At the same time, he reached to turn up the volume on the voice of Vali Tremayne.

Vali had seen him again tonight. This was the third straight evening he'd been out there, little more than a vague silhouette beyond the sea wall.

With an uneasy frown, she dropped the corner of the drapes and inched back from the window, glancing nervously around the living room. The room was usually a bright splash of color with its lemon walls and floral chintz, but now it was steeped in shadows from the dim light of a glazed table lamp. Her gaze fastened on a photograph tucked among the numerous books and ceramic bowls on the shelves beside the fireplace.

She walked across the room and with a faint, sad smile lifted the glass-covered frame from the shelf. A dark-haired man with a pleasant, appealing face laughed out at her. Gently, she touched the glass with her index finger, rubbing the surface as if she could evoke a response. *Paul...*

Almost guiltily, she set the frame back in place. Graham had wanted her to put his brother's photograph away long ago. At first, he had only suggested that she remove this last memento of her relationship with Paul. Later, suggestion had strengthened to request, but even though she didn't want to hurt Graham, she couldn't bring herself to do what he asked.

She stood staring at the photo, not touching it, but simply remembering the day it had been taken, how Paul had laughed when he'd repeated to her his agent's insistence that he adopt a more serious, thoughtful expression for his publicity photos . . .

"I'm supposed to look more—*intense*," he'd told her, drawing his face into a ridiculous caricature of stern piety that had lasted only a second before he broke into his familiar laughing countenance.

Paul, with his smiling heart and laughing eyes . . . always so happy, so confident, so hopeful. Until all the bright and wonderful things that made him Paul were destroyed in a burning plane beneath a cold, black mountain sky.

She pressed the fingertips of one hand to her temple, a reaction to the subtle pulse of pain that was beginning to throb there. It was always that way, when she let herself remember, when she allowed her thoughts to drift back to the time they'd had together, the things they had shared together, the things he had told her . . . .

No. Don't try to remember. Graham's right; she mustn't think about the past. She mustn't try to remember. Yesterday was dead, it was meant to be buried. With Paul.

Reluctantly, she turned away from the photograph and went back to the window, cautiously nudging a corner of the drapes aside and glancing out. There was no one there.

She walked through the cottage to check the locks on both doors, went into the bathroom and took a small white pill, then settled down on the couch to read Leda Alexander's newest novel.

1

"Oh, Daniel—I wish you could see the beach! It looks exactly the way I remember it." Jennifer tugged at Dan's hand to pull him along beside her, then stopped to allow Sunny, Dan's golden retriever guide dog, to do her job.

Her husband of exactly one week smiled at her excitement. "I'll see it through your eyes, love. But let me take off my shoes first, okay? I never could walk in sand with my shoes on."

Jennifer plopped down beside him on the warm sand and pulled off her own tennis shoes. She balanced on her knees for a moment to look out over Lake Erie.

Even though it was hot for September, almost muggy, the beach was dotted with only a few people. The Labor Day weekend was over, bringing an end to the annual vacation season. The few tenants and cottage owners still in the area would now be occupied with readying their cottages for winter; most of them would be gone by the end of the month.

"Glad we came?" Dan asked, pulling her to her feet with one hand.

"It means the world to me," she answered softly. "The Smokies were wonderful, but this place is so special to me, Daniel. My family brought us up here every summer until the year before Mother died." She took his tennis shoes from him and carried them with her own so he could hold Sunny's leash and still walk arm-in-arm with her.

"There's a pier not too far away from us—with a lighthouse at the end," she told him. "When I was a kid, I used to fish there with my dad."

11

It was second nature for Jennifer to help Dan see things through her eyes. For several months, she'd been working as his executive assistant at the Christian radio station he owned in West Virginia. By now she'd grown accustomed to keeping up a continual flow of casual observation to make Dan aware of what was going on around him.

He had been blinded five years before. But in spite of his handicap, Jennifer had almost immediately decided that Daniel Kaine was the most fascinating, and often baffling, man she'd ever known. Though he was somewhat over-whelming in size—he topped Jennifer's five-eight by more than half a foot, and he had the rock-hard athletic physique of a former Olympic swimming champion—he was easily the gentlest, kindest man she'd ever met.

She still marveled at his uncanny sensitivity for the feelings of other people, his sometimes disturbing directness, and his generosity of spirit that knew no limit. He also possessed, Jennifer had quickly learned, a healthy sense of mischief and a ruthless sense of humor.

In Jennifer's eyes, he was a wonderful man, a remarkable man—and she loved him more than life. She flooded Dan's world with affection, and he, in turn, openly adored her, cherished her, and made her, she was sure, the happiest woman on earth.

In addition to being a happy woman, however, Jennifer was also an acutely *curious* woman. Rousing herself from the lulling sound of waves lapping gently on the beach, she came to a sudden stop. A sprawling stone bi-level house, standing at least a hundred yards away from its nearest neighbor, caught her attention. The house was secluded almost to the point of obscurity by enormous trees and a high sea wall. Nevertheless, it presented a friendly, inviting appearance, with early fall flowers blooming all across the front beneath a huge bay window.

"I've *got* to get a closer look at this place!" she said, abruptly tugging at Dan's arm. "Come on, Daniel."

"Jennifer, don't—" Too late, Dan swerved, the retriever stopped, and Jennifer whirled around to correct her mistake. All three collided.

"Uh-oh," Jennifer muttered, looking up at Dan's face. "I did it again, didn't I?"

Dan's reply was an exaggerated wince of pain as he gingerly touched one rib.

Immediately concerned, Jennifer drew in a sharp breath of dismay. "Did I *hurt* you? Oh, Daniel, I'm *sorry*! I wasn't thinking . . . I was staring at this wonderful house—you should see it—it's really nifty—"

Dan's look of discomfort was impressively genuine as he stood unmoving, allowing her to massage his side while she continued to murmur sympathetically.

As if he could no longer contain it, he flashed a roguish grin and said mildly, "That's okay, kid. I don't suppose I can complain about your running into me when that's what brought us together in the first place."

Jennifer gave the afflicted rib a gentle shove in answer to his crack about their first meeting. "I didn't run into *you* that day, Daniel Kaine. *You* ran into me."

Still grinning, he shrugged. "Whatever. It worked." ,

"Come *on*, Daniel! I want to get a closer look at this house."

"What's so great about it?" he asked, looking a little disgruntled at being led by both his wife and his dog. He stumbled, frowned and muttered, "If you two are going to be a team, I wish you'd work the bugs out of your act."

"This place is *not* your typical lakeside cottage," Jennifer said distractedly, plowing through the sand. "It's all stone . . . and it goes on forever. And it's mysterious looking."

13

"Mysterious looking," Dan repeated dryly. "What's that mean?"

Slowing her stride, Jennifer gripped his arm a little more tightly, then started up a narrow cement walkway that led from the end of the sea wall to the front door of the house. "It has a certain—presence," she said thoughtfully. "It looks like a house with secrets."

When Dan mumbled something inaudible, Jennifer ignored him and kept on going.

She started to turn toward the right side of the house, but Daniel stopped. "Do you hear that?" He lifted his chin expectantly.

The sound of music—contemporary Christian music— came pouring out from the house. It sounded like a full-sized band, but Jennifer recognized a state-of-the-art synthesizer when she heard one. She also knew enough music to spot the technique of a professional.

"It's coming from this side of the house," Jennifer said, abruptly leading off to the right. "Let's go around where we can hear better."

Digging his feet in, Dan said, "Jennifer . . . am I right in assuming that we're tramping around private property?"

She looked at him. "We're not going to bother anyone." Again she tried to get him to move. The retriever at his side gave Jennifer a look of mild exasperation as if to convey the message that she needed no help in carrying out her job.

Dan sighed but started walking. "I'm totally dominated by two females."

"And you love it. Now come on."

A large casement window was open at the front side of the house, and Jennifer headed resolutely toward it. They stopped only a few feet away. The brilliantly executed instrumental music that was flowing and reverberating from the house was now joined by the sound of an incredibly smooth, powerful female voice—a voice with tremendous range and perfect control.

Both Dan and Jennifer stood fascinated, rooted to the spot as they listened. Dan reached for Jennifer's hand and, finding it, squeezed it gently.

It was an expert rendering of a Christian song, a song Jennifer thought must be brand new. Within the course of a week's broadcasting at the station, she probably heard all the current gospel and CCM favorites, as well as any promising new recordings. This one was new, she was sure—new and extremely good.

But it wasn't only the song that held her captive. It was the voice.

Dan, too, seemed riveted by the singer. "Jennifer . . . do you recognize that voice?" he asked in a low murmur.

"I know I should, it's awfully familiar . . . . " She drew in a sudden sharp breath. "*Daniel* . . . that sounds like . . . no, it couldn't be—"

"Tremayne," he said softly, shaking his head in wonder. "Vali Tremayne. It has to be."

"But it *can't* be," Jennifer protested stubbornly. "She hasn't sung for years. Besides, what in the world would she be doing up here?"

Dan thought a moment. "I think I remember reading that Paul Alexander was from somewhere in this area. Wasn't there some speculation after he died that Vali Tremayne came up here to live so she could be close to his family?"

"I don't remember anything like that. But I *do* remember that she quit singing."

"I'm telling you, that's her," he insisted.

Jennifer knew it was unlikely that he was mistaken; still, she found it difficult, if not impossible, to believe that they

15

were standing outside a beach house listening to Vali Tremayne.

"Didn't she have some sort of nervous breakdown before she quit?" she asked Daniel.

Paying far more attention to the music than to Jennifer, Dan nodded vaguely. "Mm-hm, but...." He paused. "Weird...."

"Weird? What's weird?"

He shook his head. "Nothing. It was just a feeling I had for a minute. Listen to that synth. Someone sure knows their stuff, huh?"

"Well, I'm going to find out who's in there," Jennifer said briskly. "Let's go to the door."

"Go to the—*Jennifer!*" He turned toward her. "We can't just go up to the door."

"Of course we can, Daniel," she said firmly, already moving toward the front of the house. "Don't worry, I won't embarrass you. We'll simply introduce ourselves and find out who—"

Her voice faltered, then caught. She stopped dead when she saw the front door open. "*Daniel*—" she hissed furtively—"somebody's coming out! Let's go back around to the side so they won't think we're snooping."

"We *are* snooping, Jennifer," Dan answered testily. "Where are you, anyway?"

She caught his arm. "Wait," she said, restraining him with her hand while she craned her neck to peer around the corner of the house.

The man stepping off the small concrete porch into the yard was tall—nearly as tall as Daniel, Jennifer thought. And like Daniel, he also wore a beard, though his was more closely trimmed. There, however, the resemblance ended.

Where Daniel's frame was powerful and thickly muscled from years of disciplined training as a swimmer, this man looked lean and wiry, almost too slender for his height. The

16

profile he presented stopped just short of being gaunt. His hair was an odd tawny shade, generously threaded with silver—in direct contrast to his darker beard. His skin was deeply tanned, and as he walked out into the yard Jennifer could see that he had a slight, but noticeable limp, as if his right leg were somewhat stiff.

It was his voice, however, that made her eyes widen with curiosity. He spoke in a hoarse, strained whisper as he turned to the open doorway.

"Vali, I don't see her anywhere. Maybe you'd better come out and call her."

Both Jennifer and Daniel jumped, reacting not only to the strange whisper of a voice but to the name he had called the woman. Jennifer's eyes followed the direction of the stranger's gaze, and she expelled a soft little sound of amazement.

Framed in the doorway of the house stood a slight young woman with a lovely, patrician face, a face as familiar to most Christians as her voice.

Jennifer locked her hand on Dan's forearm and squeezed.

"Dan—it's *her*! It's Vali Tremayne!" Too stunned with excitement to be discreet, she blurted out her words without thinking, then turned crimson with embarrassment when both the woman in the doorway and the light-haired man whirled around in surprise.

2

"Ah . . . hello," Jennifer stammered weakly.

There was no reply. Vali Tremayne's expression wasn't hostile, only curious. But the man appraised the Kaines with a speculative, none-too-friendly stare that added a touch of unease to Jennifer's embarrassment.

Obviously, the present circumstances called for an explanation. Just as obviously, Daniel had no intention of offering that explanation.

"We were just . . . ah . . . taking a walk." She paused, waited, and tried again. "I noticed your house—it's just lovely—and wanted to get a closer look at it. There aren't many places along the beach nearly as nice as this . . . that's why it caught my attention. You see, I used to come up here all the time, so I remember things pretty well, but I knew I hadn't seen your home before."

She was becoming faintly unnerved by the blond man's skeptical stare and a little irritated with Daniel's deliberate silence. Her words spilled out even faster. "I was telling Daniel—this is Daniel—" she tugged at his arm to coax him closer—"how attractive your home is. Oh, I'm Jennifer. Jennifer Kaine. We're on our honeymoon, you see. We've been married a week now."

She glanced at Daniel, then did a double take when she saw that he was positively cringing at her explanation.

"I'm terribly sorry," she said, determined to redeem herself and feeling a small flicker of hope when she saw a ghost of a smile touch Vali Tremayne's lips. "I suppose you think we're trespassing—actually, we *are* trespassing, I know. But we couldn't resist your music. Daniel owns a radio station—it's a Christian station, by the way—and he

18

recognized your voice, Miss Tremayne. I told him it couldn't be you, but . . . . "

"Jennifer . . . " Daniel's voice was pleasantly soft, unmistakably firm, and enormously welcome. Jennifer drew in a long breath of relief; he would take charge now. She smiled at Vali Tremayne, then at the tall, tense-looking man who had gone to stand a little closer to the singer. She noticed that he made no effort to return her smile.

"It's my fault, I'm afraid," Daniel said with great charm. As he spoke, Sunny sat calmly but alertly beside him, staring at the two strangers as if to punctuate the fact that her owner was her personal responsibility. "I'm probably one of your most faithful fans, Miss Tremayne, and I simply had to find out for myself if that incomparable voice was real or recorded."

He thrust his right hand forward as if he knew exactly where the others were standing. "As my wife said, I'm Daniel Kaine. And this is a real pleasure."

Jennifer watched him closely, suppressing the desire to roll her eyes. Her gaze then moved to the other man. She watched him flick his dark gray eyes from Daniel to Sunny, then back again to Daniel's face. Apparently, he had just realized that Daniel was blind. His expression gradually relaxed, and the look of suspicion faded as he quickly stepped toward Dan to shake his hand.

At the same time, Vali Tremayne ran a slender hand through her incredible hair—her incredible *mahogany* hair, Jennifer thought with admiration—and smiled uncertainly with what appeared to be a touch of shyness.

Jennifer quickly returned her attention to Daniel and the other man when she heard his odd, whispering voice.

"I'm David Nathan Keye," he said, studying Dan's face with keen interest as they shook hands. "And I believe you already know that this is Vali Tremayne," he added, nodding his head in the singer's direction.

Jennifer had a fleeting impression of something slightly off balance in the man's face, then realized that his left eye had just a faint droop, as if it were heavier than the right. She thought he was an interesting looking man. She sensed a kind of melancholy about him, oddly contrasted with what looked to be a glint of mischief in his eyes. He was attractive enough, she supposed; the light hair was a surprising accent to his dark skin, and overall his features were strong and pleasant. In spite of his appeal, however, Jennifer felt a certain ambiguity in the man that instinctively put her on guard.

His next words surprised her. "You're not by any chance a composer?" he asked Dan.

Hesitating a fraction of a moment, Dan answered, "I run a Christian radio station. But *you're* a composer," he quickly added. "And an impressive one. I know your music."

Keye looked surprised, but continued to study Dan. "There's a Daniel Kaine who wrote an absolutely wonderful musical drama called *Daybreak*," he said in his peculiar whispering voice. "I believe he's . . . blind also. That's why I asked if you're a composer—I thought perhaps . . . ."

Unable to contain herself an instant longer, Jennifer exclaimed with pride, "That's Daniel! He wrote *Daybreak*!"

Keye's facial expression brightened to a genuine look of pleased admiration. Without hesitating, he gripped Daniel's hand again, this time shaking it more vigorously. "I've wanted to meet you since the first time I heard the score of *Daybreak*, just to tell you I think it's the most powerful piece of contemporary Christian music I've ever heard."

By now Jennifer had decided that Keye's peculiar voice wasn't merely a static occurrence but a permanent handicap, and she wondered what had caused it. When he again turned his attention to her, she was surprised to see that there was a faint glow of warmth in his eyes. "And are you a musician, too, Mrs. Kaine?"

"Goodness, no! I'm—"

"A fantastic singer . . . and a terrific wife," Daniel finished for her.

"I'm *not*," Jennifer quickly protested. When Dan laughed, she glanced from him to Keye. "I mean, I hope I'm a good wife," she said, flustered, "but don't listen to anything else he says."

"Why don't we go inside and have some coffee?' the composer suggested. "Vali and I were just about to take a break when we noticed Trouble had disappeared again."

"Trouble?" Jennifer repeated blankly.

The singer spoke for the first time since their encounter, explaining softly, "My cat. Her name is Trouble."

"And she wears it well," Keye added sardonically. "Come on in," he offered, starting toward the porch.

"David . . . if they're on their honeymoon," Vali said uncertainly, "perhaps they'd rather not . . . . "

The composer looked from Vali to Jennifer. "Sorry," he said with an unexpectedly boyish grin. Reaching into the pocket of his striped shirt, he pulled out a stick of gum. The guarded cynicism so evident in his expression a few minutes before seemed to have totally vanished. He tucked the gum into his mouth, still smiling at Vali. Jennifer saw a hint of an emotion that could only be tenderness in his eyes when he looked at the small young woman standing next to him. "I wasn't thinking."

"But we'd love to come in," Jennifer said quickly. "Wouldn't we, Daniel?"

Dan opened his mouth to say something but seemed to change his mind. With a knowing smile, he nodded. "Sure. Is this your home?" he asked Keye.

"I rent it." The composer took Vali's arm as they stepped back onto the porch and held the door for Dan and Jennifer to enter.

"Do you mind my dog?" Dan asked him.

"Not at all," Keye assured him. "What's his name?"

"*Her* name," Daniel corrected. "Her name is Sunny." He pursed his lips. "We'd better put our shoes on, Jennifer, before we go inside."

"Not necessary," Keye said with a smile. "My place is ever so humble. Just come as you are."

He waited for Sunny to guide Daniel through the doorway, then followed the others into a large, comfortably furnished living room dominated by a walnut grand piano and a bank of digital synthesizers. The room was clean but cluttered. Stacks of music manuscripts were everywhere; the rack on the piano was covered with staff paper and notebooks; and an empty coffee cup seemed to be on every table.

The composer crossed the room and took an indifferent swipe at the heap of staff paper and magazines on a table in front of the modular couch. "The place is messy but rat-free," he said over his shoulder. "Let's go into the kitchen; it's probably cleaner, since I seldom use it. Say, you didn't see a slightly weird-looking cat anywhere, did you? Looks a bit like a confused, overweight rabbit with stubby ears?"

"I'm afraid not," Jennifer said, laughing at him.

"David keeps hoping she'll just vanish," Vali told them with a scolding glance at the composer. "The two of them have been at war since the first day they met."

"That was no meeting," Keye said archly. "That was a duel."

"She's only a kitten," Vali protested.

"With the heart of a cheetah," he returned, leading the way into a large, country kitchen with an adjoining glassed-in sun room.

Looking around, Jennifer wondered about the relationship between Vali Tremayne and David Nathan Keye. As Daniel had, she'd recognized the composer's name right away. Not only had he written many of the hit songs on the Christian music charts, but he was a well-known keyboard artist as well. And he was obviously, her romantic spirit suggested, quite taken with the young singer standing at the kitchen counter pouring coffee. Remembering the tragic death of Vali's fiance, Paul Alexander, and the numerous references to her inconsolable grief, Jennifer found herself hoping that Vali had found someone else.

In a surprisingly brief time, the four of them fell into an easy, companionable conversation, sitting around the small oval table in the spacious kitchen, drinking coffee and talking as casually as if they'd known each other for years.

Jennifer could hear the respect in Dan's voice when he spoke to Keye. "You've got music all over the charts right now, David. You must write in your sleep."

The composer took a tray of cookies from Vali and brought it to the table, then straddled a chair. "I wish I could." He bit into a cookie before saying, "My music is my way of trying to communicate the Lord's love, His majesty, His . . . . " He stopped, then added, "Obviously, this isn't the voice of a preacher. So I write music. Vali, however, insists that I'm a workaholic." His smile was soft as he watched the singer pull up a chair beside him.

"He doesn't know when to quit," Vali explained, glancing at Jennifer. "But if I could write music like David's, I probably wouldn't want to stop either."

Jennifer stared at her, struck by Vali's flawless features. She remembered seeing pictures of her from years past. But she now realized the publicity photos hadn't begun to reveal the singer's almost ethereal loveliness.

Her face was an exquisitely contoured oval; her skin had a translucent quality; and her jade-colored eyes dominated her face with a haunting sadness that made it difficult to look away from her. And her hair—*that wonderful, incredible hair*, Jennifer thought—was an untamed cloud that formed a swirling, dramatic contrast to the delicate perfection of her

4 016 9

face. She looked, Jennifer thought fancifully, like an exiled princess, even in the yellow pin-striped jumpsuit she was wearing. She had heard Keye refer to her as "princess" a couple of times during their conversation and had smiled at the appropriateness of the pet name.

Suddenly aware that she was staring, Jennifer turned her attention to Daniel, who was sitting beside her.

"Are you recording again, Miss Tremayne?" he asked.

The singer stared at him for a moment with a slightly troubled frown. "Please . . . call me Vali. I . . . I don't know, about recording, I mean. It's been . . . a long time. David has been working with me on some arrangements, but I haven't . . . made any real decision yet."

She had a peculiar, static way of speaking, Jennifer noticed, that signaled a kind of uncertainty, a reluctance to assert herself. Combined with the faint hint of bewilderment in her eyes, she gave off an aura of skittishness, much like a young animal about to bolt.

"What Vali is much too polite to tell you," Keye quickly inserted, "is that her agent more or less strong-armed her into working with me. You see, a lot of people—myself at the top of the list—want to see Vali back in the industry. My producer and I are trying to sell her on the idea of using my music as her return vehicle."

When Vali continued to stare absently at the tabletop, Daniel said lightly, "After what Jennifer and I heard today, I'd say that's a great idea."

Keye was studying Vali with concern and seemed reluctant to look away from her when Dan spoke again.

"You've been doing a lot of keyboard work for a number of artists, haven't you? In addition to your own composing, I mean?"

"Actually, that's what gave me my start when I came here from the coast," Keye replied. "A few people knew my keyboard work from California and got me some miscellaneous jobs in Nashville. Eventually I was able to use my keyboard connections to get some of my own music recorded."

"You're from California, then?" Daniel asked.

"For the most part." The composer flashed a brief smile, then let the conversation drop for a moment as he poured himself another cup of coffee. "Until October, at least, I'm a Buckeye. My rent is paid until then."

"Jennifer's a Buckeye," Dan said, smiling in her direction. "A transplanted one, that is. She's learning to become a Mountaineer now."

"You're from . . . let's see . . . Mountaineer—that's West Virginia, right?" the composer asked.

"Shepherd Valley," Dan replied. "Just a little town at the foot of some great mountains."

"And you own a Christian radio station? That means you're one of the fellows who can help make or break my career."

Dan laughed easily. "I'm afraid we don't have that kind of influence. But you don't have anything to worry about— you're well on your way."

"That may depend on whether or not I can get Vali to sing my music," Keye said, turning to look at the singer.

His remark disturbed Jennifer; she thought it sounded as if the composer intended to use Vali. She knew it was none of her business, but something about the quiet young singer inspired her protective instincts.

Unexpectedly, Vali smiled at him. "David, you make it sound as if I had to be forced to work with you."

Keye shrugged, but the smile he gave her was gentle. "My rent's only paid until October, princess. I'm running out of time to come up with that one special number you simply can't resist."

"Well, you'll certainly be doing all of us a big favor," Daniel said to Keye, "if you can get her back into a recording studio."

The composer nodded. "There's a whole host of people out there who agree with you, Daniel." His gaze suddenly focused on something outside the kitchen window. "Unfortunately," he said, "you're about to meet someone who doesn't."

His whispered comment was sharply punctuated by a loud, demanding knock on the side door. At the same time, Sunny roused from her place by Dan's chair with a warning growl, then stood waiting alertly at his side. Dan reached to gentle her with his hand and a soft word of reassurance.

Before the last thud died away, a big, sandy-haired man pushed through the door, stepping into the kitchen as if he had an unquestioned right to enter without being invited. He stood staring at the four of them through narrow, pale gray eyes. He looked impatient, surprised, and angry.

Without getting up, David gave him a cool smile and said, his whisper-voice even rougher than before, "Won't you come in, Graham?"

Jennifer couldn't take her eyes off the man, inexplicably finding his handsome features vaguely familiar. Nearly as tall as the other two men in the room, he looked to be about fifteen pounds heavier than Daniel—a little overweight, she thought. She guessed him to be in his early to mid-thirties. His well-tailored gray suit looked almost comically out of place, considering their lakefront surroundings. She had the sudden impression of a somewhat stuffy, imperious man.

He flicked a brief, disdainful glance at David, then frowned at Vali. "You might let me know when you're going to be away from your cottage for such a long time, Vali. I've been trying to call you for well over two hours now." His voice was refined, clipped, almost British in nuance.

Jennifer flinched in surprise when Vali stood, pushing her

chair back so abruptly it almost toppled.

"Oh, Graham—I'm so sorry! David and I were working on some new numbers . . . and then we met Daniel and Jennifer—" She stopped, glanced for an instant at Jennifer, then turned back to the man now towering over her. "I just didn't think . . . ."

He cast a withering look at Keye, then stared hard at Dan and Jennifer before returning his attention to Vali. "That's becoming somewhat of a habit with you these days, isn't it, dear?" he asked icily.

Vali colored and bit her lower lip. Jennifer saw that she was wringing her hands almost desperately. "I . . . should have called you. I forgot."

"I should think by now you'd know how I worry about you, Vali."

"Yes . . . I do know, Graham . . . ." The pretty singer's voice had softened until it was almost as much of a whisper as Keye's.

The composer now stood, his eyes glinting with an unpleasant look of challenge. "It was my fault, Graham—as usual," he rasped. "I'm afraid I have a tendency to forget everything else but . . . the music . . . when I'm working with Vali."

When the other man remained silent, Keye continued. "Let me introduce you to Daniel and Jennifer Kaine, Graham. Fellow musicians—and new friends."

The man turned to study the Kaines as David continued.

"Daniel, Jennifer—this is Graham Alexander. A very . . . close friend of Vali's."

Graham Alexander! Jennifer almost choked. This man was the twin brother of Paul Alexander, Vali's deceased fiance. There had been a lot of publicity at the time of the famous musician's death, including a number of references to his brother, a research scientist, and his mother, an internationally known novelist. Staring hard at the big man

27

with the chilling eyes, Jennifer was surprised she hadn't seen the resemblance immediately. The man standing across the table from her looked enough like his dead brother to be mistaken for him, except for the extra pounds he was carrying.

Graham Alexander offered only a small, formal nod in acknowledgment of the introduction. Brusquely turning to Vali, he said, "You *did* remember that we're meeting Mother at the Twine House for dinner?"

"Oh, of course," she replied. "I hadn't forgotten."

His measuring gaze swept over her, and Jennifer felt a pang of sympathy for the lovely young singer when he asked pointedly, "You'll be changing into something more suitable, I imagine?"

Vali looked at him blankly, then glanced down at her slightly rumpled jumpsuit. "Oh . . . yes. This isn't . . . I wasn't going to wear this."

David now crossed his arms over his chest and stared at the gray-suited Alexander. "The Twine House is formal?" He freed one hand to place it alongside his bearded cheek. "And to think," he said, wide-eyed with an expression of mock humiliation, "I went there in my jeans last night. It's a wonder they didn't toss me out."

The scientist settled a look of contempt on Keye, his silent glare making a statement of its own.

David shrugged. "Ah, well . . . what would you expect from a beach bum musician, right, Graham?"

If his mocking grin had been meant to needle the other man, it had the intended effect. Alexander scowled, smoothed the knot of his silk tie, and turned to Vali.

"I'll pick you up at six. We're to meet Mother at six-fifteen." Without waiting for an answer, he pecked her lightly on the cheek, cast one more scathing look of distaste at David, then turned and went out the door, closing it with a firm thud behind him.

It was quiet in the kitchen for a long, awkward moment after he left. Vali was obviously embarrassed, and Jennifer could sense the tension in David, who continued to stare gloomily after Graham Alexander for a long time.

It was Daniel who finally broke the silence. "We should be going, Jennifer," he said, standing and reaching for her hand. "We haven't even unpacked all our stuff yet."

Keye and Vali followed them outside, where they stood talking for a few more moments. Jennifer was surprised when Dan started to shake hands with the composer, then stopped and asked, "I wonder . . . would the two of you mind if I looked at you? With my hands?" He smiled ingenuously. "To tell you the truth, it's a little more than a blind man's curiosity. I thought it would be something to tell my kids some day."

Jennifer was surprised when Vali stepped up to him without hesitating. "Your children probably won't know who you're talking about, Daniel," she said softly, "but go right ahead."

As Dan explored the lovely face at his fingertips, Jennifer smiled, remembering his gentleness the first time he had "looked" at her.

After he dropped his hands back to his side, Daniel smiled and said, "David, I'll just bet you're not that pretty."

The composer's eyes narrowed for an instant as he studied Dan. Jennifer thought she sensed a fleeting look of anxiety in his expression, but he covered it with a brief smile. "A keenly accurate assumption, Daniel." His voiceless laugh sounded forced and nervous, and he bore Dan's examination of his face with obvious reluctance.

Jennifer was puzzled by her husband's questioning frown as he finally let his hands drop away from Keye's face.

"It's always interesting to me, you know, when I finally put a face with a voice," Dan said casually. "You surprised me, David. I pictured you without a beard—and a little heavier."

Keye lifted one eyebrow skeptically. "What? Not Quasimodo?"

Now Dan frowned in earnest.

The composer laughed. "The voice, man. It gets to people, you know."

"What caused it?" Dan asked him directly.

Keye shrugged. "Accident. My vocal chords were crushed." He paused, then added, "I read about what happened to you in some of the news releases when *Daybreak* was first released. A drunk driver, wasn't it?"

Dan nodded slowly, looking as if he were about to say something else. Instead, he stooped to put Sunny's leash on her, then straightened and shook hands with Keye. After a few more minutes of goodbyes, he and Jennifer started back down the walkway toward the beach.

Later that night, they walked hand-in-hand along the shore, allowing Sunny to run free. The air was still warm, as yet holding no hint of the approaching autumn that usually came early to northern Ohio. It was quiet and serene, the kind of night made for hushed voices, soft music, and quiet laughter.

"What do you think of our new acquaintances?" Daniel asked as they walked along.

Jennifer didn't answer right away. "I'm not sure," she finally said. "They're . . . unusual."

After a long pause, Daniel asked, "How old would you guess David to be?"

"Oh . . . I don't know. He's one of those people who looks young one minute and older the next. Early thirties at least. He has a good bit of gray in his hair, but it's mixed in with blond, so you don't really notice it at first." She paused. "What did you think of him?"

He shrugged. "I'm not sure. For some reason, I found him difficult to visualize." After a moment, he said, "There's

30

something . . . peculiar about his skin."

"Peculiar? What do you mean?"

"It's . . . not elastic enough for a man his age." He gave a short laugh. "I know it sounds crazy, but he has the skin of a teenager. And around his hairline . . . . " He didn't finish.

"His hairline?"

He laughed again and shook his head. "I must be losing my touch."

Jennifer looked at him, then groaned. "If that was a pun, you've done better, Daniel."

He grinned. "Humor me." He stroked his chin, then asked stubbornly, "You're sure he's in his thirties?"

"At least. Really, Daniel."

"Hmm. His left eye droops a little, doesn't it?"

She glanced up at him with amusement. "You don't miss much, do you? Yes, as a matter of fact, it does. Not a lot, just enough to make him look rather . . . cunning."

"Cunning. That's a detective story word, kid. What do you mean?"

She considered. "Smart. A little devious, I think. But nice." She hesitated. "That's the strange thing about him . . . . "

"What's that, love?"

"He's puzzling. Overall, he seems to be very nice, good-natured, charming—definitely intelligent. But there's something else that doesn't quite fit, and I'm not sure what it is."

"Explosive."

"What?" She was only half-listening. "Let's stop here a minute, Daniel. I've got a stone or something in my sandal."

"I'd guess he's under a great deal of stress," Dan said thoughtfully.

"Mmm. He limps . . . did I tell you?" She pulled a small stone from the toe of her sandal. "Just a little—like his leg is stiff."

Sunny came bounding up to them just then, and Dan

31

stooped to rub her ears, then straightened. "And the lovely Vali is like . . . a frightened little fawn," he remarked.

Jennifer drew in a sharp gasp of agreement. "That's exactly what she makes me think of! I couldn't have been any more surprised by her, Daniel. You hear her sing, and you get this fantastic sense of power and control. But in person, she's actually . . . *timid*, I think."

They started walking again. "And what about Graham Alexander?" Jennifer asked, linking her arm with his. "Do you suppose they're engaged? I didn't see a ring."

"He certainly seems to have some sort of hold on her, doesn't he?"

"I thought he was insufferable. What kind of vibes did *you* get about him?"

He grimaced. "I don't get *vibes*, Jennifer. I'm blind, not psychic."

"Ooh, touchy." She grinned at him, savoring the way the soft puffs of wind off the lake lifted strands of his charcoal-dark hair, ruffling it and tossing it gently over his forehead. "But what did you think of him?"

His tone was puzzled when he answered. "I'm not sure. They're an interesting trio, aren't they?"

"Well, I can tell you one thing—David is in love with Vali," she said firmly.

Dan came to an abrupt halt, and a ghost of a smile flickered across his face. Still smiling, he gathered her into his arms. "And Daniel," he said softly, "is in love with Jennifer." Without warning, he lowered his head to kiss her lightly, then again, this time not so lightly.

"*Daniel* . . . " Her protest was weak. "There are people on the beach . . . "

"Then what we need to do," he murmured against her cheek, "is get off the beach."

3

The man was almost asleep when the demanding shrill of the bedside phone shattered the silence. He bolted upright in the darkness, and reached for the receiver.

"Who are they?"

Groggy, he was slow to react. "They?"

The voice on the other end of the line sounded impatient. "The blind man and the woman—who are they?"

He looked at the digital clock on the night table. It was twenty minutes after midnight. "Kaine. Daniel and Jennifer Kaine. There's no problem with them—they'll be gone in a few days."

"Anyone new could be a problem at this time."

"I hardly think we need to feel threatened by a blind man and his wife." The man's voice dripped sarcasm.

There was silence for a moment. Then, "Only the singer is a threat. And, as you've so confidently assured us, the solution to that particular problem is forthcoming." The voice roughened even more. "May I ask again . . . *when*?"

The man sighed, trying for patience. "Soon. I need a few more weeks, I told you."

"No. One week, no more. You've already wasted far too much time with her."

"Everything is working out exactly as I planned. She remembers nothing, and I've become very important to her. The rest is a matter of time."

"No, my friend. Either you have a definite solution, a commitment, within the next week, or we eliminate her." After a slight hesitation the voice, softer now but still ominously suggestive, added, "Which is what we should have done in the first place."

"That is, and always has been, an extremely foolish idea. She's far too well known, and it would simply be too much of a coincidence after the airplane crash. No," he said decisively, "my way is better. You'll see."

"Well . . . we shall hope that you are proven right. In the meantime, we'll be helping you however we can."

"What do you mean?"

"Simply that the more disoriented and confused she grows, the more dependent upon you she will become."

"I can handle this alone," the man said sharply.

"Of course, you can. But we're in this together, are we not? The least I can do is to lend you a bit of assistance."

"I'm warning you, if you do something to ruin what I've accomplished so far—"

"Do not warn me of *anything*, my friend." The voice was soft, the threat implicit, the click of the phone final.

Only after he replaced the receiver did the man finally switch on the lamp. He sat on the side of the bed for a few more minutes, then stood. With a scowling glance at the telephone, he threw on a bathrobe and stalked out of the room. One week. Not a long time. But it would have to be enough.

4

"I really respect your courage, darlin'," Dan said with a wondering shake of his head. "But doesn't the idea of me in an amusement park remind you of Daniel in the lions' den?"

Jennifer poured him a second cup of coffee and refilled her own cup before sitting down at the table beside him. "As I recall," she said pointedly, "*that* Daniel got out without a scratch."

"Amusement parks close after Labor Day, love," he said mildly, reaching for his third doughnut.

"But Cedar Point is open for two weekends *after* Labor Day. And this happens to be the last weekend. Come on, Daniel, I really want to go. It'll be fun."

"Fun for who?"

"Fun for *whom*. Will you go?"

"Absolutely not."

She sighed. "I've wanted to go back to Cedar Point for years." Her voice was soft, a plaintive catch making it huskier than usual. "It would make this week even more special."

"Ah . . . sentimentality. Nice touch, kid. But I'm still not going."

She poked him.

"Jennifer, you wouldn't want me to think that the success of our honeymoon depends on me making a fool of myself at an amusement park, would you?" He swallowed a bite of his chocolate-covered doughnut.

"Since when are you intimidated by a new adventure?" she challenged him. "Daniel, I can still remember how amazed I was—and impressed—when I first started working with you and discovered how different you were from what

35

I'd expected."

He finished his doughnut, wiped the chocolate from his mouth, and leaned back in his chair. Crossing his arms comfortably over his chest, he smiled—a wide, knowing smile that plainly said he knew what was coming but wanted to hear it anyway.

"Why, I distinctly remember, Daniel, being totally dumbfounded at the way you handled things. I mean, I'd always had the idea that people with handicaps are somewhat . . . insecure."

He nodded wisely.

"But you were so extraverted and authoritative, so confident and willing to try new things—you shattered every preconceived notion I'd ever had."

He made a brief, self-deprecating gesture with his hand. "Aw, shucks, honey . . . . "

"In fact," she went on, ignoring him, "*you* made *me* feel inhibited sometimes, you were so willing to take a chance, eager to try new experiences . . . . "

Laughing, he put up a restraining hand. "This is good, darlin'—not one of your better routines, but still good."

She snarled at him, then studied his face hopefully. "Are you thinking about it, Daniel?"

"Mm. Maybe."

When he began to drum his fingers on the table, she was pretty sure she'd won.

"Does this place have a roller coaster?" he suddenly asked, stopping his rhythmic tapping.

"Does it have—Daniel, Cedar Point just happens to have more roller coasters than any other amusement park in the country," she announced smugly. "*Seven* of them, actually." She paused. "But you wouldn't want to ride a roller coaster, would you? I mean, wouldn't that be kind of scary when you can't see anything?"

He grinned wickedly. "It's what you *can* see that terrifies

36

you on a roller coaster, kid. Okay," he said decisively. "We'll go. And"—there was a significant pause—"we will ride all seven roller coasters. Together." He crossed his arms over his chest again, his smile daring her to refuse.

"I . . . ah . . . actually, I've never been on a roller coaster, Daniel."

His grin became a full-scale smirk. "Jennifer," he drawled, sitting forward on his chair and rubbing his hands together with obvious eagerness, "this is going to be a truly unforgettable day in your life."

The day couldn't have been more perfect for their plans. The temperature was in the low seventies, the air was dry, and the sky looked like frosted blue glass.

"It's going to be *extremely* crowded," Jennifer remarked as she craned her neck to study the long lines waiting at the entry gates. "There must be dozens of people ahead of us."

"Just don't lose me in the crowd," Dan said.

Hearing what sounded like an edge of anxiety in his voice, Jennifer glanced up at him. "Does it bother you a lot, being without Sunny? I didn't think we'd be able to go on the rides if she came with us."

"I don't especially like crowds, even with Sunny," he admitted. "It's too easy to get confused."

She frowned, dismayed at her own thoughtlessness. "Oh, Daniel, I'm sorry! I was so intent on having my own way I didn't even stop to think how difficult this might be for you. Listen, we don't have to go in—we'll leave right now."

He covered her hand on his forearm with his own. "No way, kid. If you think I'm going to miss a chance to ride seven roller coasters in one day, think again."

She thought his smile might be a little forced. "Daniel, are you *sure*?"

"Absolutely. I can't wait to—"

Jennifer whirled around and Dan, too, turned his head in surprise when a harsh whisper rasped their names from behind. Standing off to one side of the line was Vali Tremayne, accompanied by David Nathan Keye, who smiled and waved what looked like a handful of passes.

"I can get all of us in on these," he said. "Let me treat you, okay?"

Without waiting for a reply, he and Vali walked over. Keye touched Dan lightly on the shoulder in a friendly gesture, then linked arms with both Jennifer and Vali as he began to move around the line and up to the entry gate. Jennifer held Dan's hand tightly so they didn't get separated.

Once through the gate, after thanking Keye for their free admission, Jennifer turned to Vali and said, "So you decided to take advantage of this last weekend, too?"

"I twisted her arm," David said with a grin as he tucked a piece of gum into his mouth. "I love amusement parks. And I figured if this one is so great that I heard about it n California, it must really be something."

"You won't be disappointed, David," Jennifer told him, glancing about their surroundings. "Oh, look—here comes the clown band!"

A parade of wildly dressed, zany clowns came strutting down a nearby lane, playing a variety of instruments and shouting among themselves.

After they passed, David took Vali by the hand and looked thoughtfully from Dan to Jennifer. "Say, you two wouldn't want to pair up with us for the day, would you?"

"David—" Vali quickly objected—"they're on their honeymoon, remember?"

"Oh—right. Sorry; of course you'd rather be alone—"

Jennifer elbowed Dan, who flinched, then responded to his cue. "No, that sounds good to us. Jennifer?"

She shook her head eagerly. "We'd love to!"

Vali searched Jennifer's eyes. "Are you sure? We'd

understand if you'd rather not."

"No, really—it'll be fun."

"Well, then, what are we waiting for?" David studied Dan for a moment, then asked matter-of-factly, "What's easiest for you, Dan? Walking on the outside or in between us?"

Daniel replied without hesitating. "The outside, with Jennifer guiding me. She's not too good at it," he added dryly, "but I guess I can't be particular today." Jennifer dug him lightly in the ribs, and they started off.

Over the next two hours, they rode the train; ate french fries; rode the log ride; ate hot dogs; rode the Tilt-a-Whirl; ate cotton candy; rode the dodge'em cars; and ate pizza.

"I'm going to be sick," David groaned, rubbing at a dab of tomato sauce on the front of his awning-striped shirt, then pitching his napkin into a nearby trash receptacle.

"You deserve to be," Vali told him.

Jennifer didn't miss the soft-spoken singer's faint blush— of pleasure, she thought—when David hugged her to his side and said, "Have a little pity, princess. I'm turning green."

"What we need," Daniel announced, "is a change of pace. A nice leisurely ride that won't stir up or dislocate anything."

"Wise counsel, Daniel." The composer adjusted the sunglasses on the bridge of his nose with one finger.

"We'll have to bring Jason up here next year," Dan said, as they started walking again.

"He'd love it," Jennifer agreed.

"Jason?" Vali gave them a questioning look.

"Our son."

David threw them a somewhat startled glance.

"We have an adopted son," Jennifer explained. "Well, almost adopted. It won't be final for a few months yet. Dan was getting ready to adopt Jason before we got married, so now we're finalizing it in both our names."

"How old is he?" asked Vali.

"Almost nine," Jennifer answered. "And he's absolutely adorable." She already missed the small, slightly retarded towhead who had charmed his way into her heart from the very first time she'd seen him. He was staying with Dan's parents during Dan and Jennifer's wedding trip.

"Well, Daniel—what nice, leisurely ride do you recommend for us?" David asked as the four of them started to walk again.

Dan considered the question. "The ferris wheel, I think."

"Oh, no!" Jennifer said, a little too quickly.

"Oh, no?" repeated her husband.

"It's too . . . high."

"Are you afraid of heights, Jennifer?" Vali looked genuinely concerned.

"She won't admit it, but she is," Dan told them.

"I wouldn't say I'm *afraid*, exactly."

"What, then—exactly?" Dan stuck one hand in his jeans pocket and waited.

"Well . . . "

Jennifer thought Dan's smile was a little smug when he challenged her. "I thought you believed in confronting your fears."

"There's no fear to confront here, Daniel," she snapped. "I simply don't want to get on an airborne tinker toy while my stomach feels like a cement mixer. Not all of us," she said pointedly, "have steel tubing for a digestive tract."

His grin broadened. "From what you've told me, it'll come in real handy when I have to start eating your cooking."

She muttered under her breath, then said reluctantly, "Oh, all right. We'll ride the ferris wheel. But don't say I didn't warn you."

Vali stood waiting in line, vaguely wishing Jennifer hadn't

agreed to "confront her fears." Actually, she didn't much like these things either. But she found herself more likely to keep quiet about her own fears—surely far more numerous and varied than Jennifer Kaine's—when she was with David. For some inexplicable reason, she didn't want him seeing what Graham called her *neuroses*. David obviously thought well of her. Lately she'd been surprised by how much she wanted to keep his respect.

They had become good friends in these past few weeks of working together. At least, *she* counted *him* as a friend. For his part, he made her a little uncomfortable sometimes by hinting—strongly—that he was attracted to her as a woman, not only as a friend. He was recklessly candid about it, too, even in Graham's presence, unfortunately. At times he seemed to be deliberately *goading* Graham.

Last night, once he'd learned that Graham would be in Cleveland for two days, he'd become disconcertingly blunt about his feelings.

"You're not engaged to the man, right?" he'd asked directly.

"Not exactly, but—"

"I don't see a ring, Vali."

"He's asked me to marry him."

"And have you answered him?"

"Well, I have to be . . . sure."

"And you're not?"

"I—almost . . . "

"Almost doesn't count, princess."

"*David*—"

They'd been sitting beside each other on the piano bench, and he had flashed that impish grin of his and cuffed her lightly on the chin with a gentle fist. But suddenly his charcoal gray eyes had lost their sharp glint of mischief, darkening to an expression that made Vali's heart lurch and threaten to betray her loyalty to Graham. He had dropped his hands to her shoulders and held her captive with a searching, demanding look. "Vali . . . surely you know that you've become very important to me. Give me a chance, princess . . . that's all I'm asking . . . just a chance."

Without really understanding why, she'd become almost angry with him. It was as if she resented him for threatening her orderly lifestyle. She had pushed him away, then jumped up off the piano bench. "I won't work with you if you're going to act like this!"

He'd apologized at once—but only for upsetting her. Not for being interested in her. And he still looked at her . . . that way . . . the way that said he cared about her. Deeply.

He unnerved her, irritated her, almost frightened her with his intensity. And yet she trusted him. Why was that, she wondered? How could she trust such a troublesome, stubborn, impudent man? A man so different from Graham. Graham was so strong, so dependable, so . . . in control.

"Penny for them, princess," he whispered at her side.

She jumped guiltily, then locked gazes with him, caught off guard as always by the affection in his eyes.

Laughing weakly, she told him, "I'm afraid I was wishing Jennifer weren't so brave . . . about facing her fears."

His expression quickly sobered. "We don't have to go on this thing if you'd rather not."

"No—I'm just . . . a little jittery, I suppose." She brightened and smiled at him. "We came to do it all, remember?"

He slipped one long arm around her shoulders to move her through the gate. "Here we go then."

Vali stepped into the gondola, uncomfortably aware that the operator was staring curiously at her. After getting into the seat, she glanced up at the man's face, unsettled by what appeared to be a glint of amusement in his darkly shadowed eyes. Quickly, she looked away.

Dan and Jennifer were in the car just above them, and Vali could hear them laughing as the car began to move. *What a*

42

special pair they are, she thought with a smile. That wonderful, incredible blind man made her feel oddly secure and sheltered by the steady, warm strength of his presence, as did his lovely Jennifer, with her laughing dark eyes, ready wit, and totally unaffected concern for others.

"I love to see you smile like that," David told her. He still had his arm around her, and now he gently squeezed her shoulder. "But I'm almost jealous because I don't know why you're smiling."

"The Kaines," she said simply, looking out over the park. I was thinking about how special they are."

"Ah, there goes my ego again. I was hoping you were thinking of me."

"David, you are impossible," she scolded, captured by the smile in his eyes when she turned to look at him.

Disturbed by her own feelings, she quickly looked away to scan the crowd below. As they began to ascend, she caught sight of what she thought was a familiar face and stared harder.

A man, completely bald, stood motionless in the throng of people at the base of the ride. Vali was certain he was staring up at her. Not tall, but square and somewhat heavy, he had the thick, over-muscled appearance of a boxer past his prime. In a conservative dark suit, he looked grossly out of place in his surroundings.

The sight of him discomfited her, for she felt a slight sense of recognition as she looked at him, yet she was positive she had never seen him before. David said something to her just then, and by the time she glanced back into the crowd, the man had disappeared.

She was still trying to place him in her memory as they climbed to the top. Suddenly a loud crunch threw her against the safety bar, and the ride came to an abrupt stop. She knew it was Jennifer who cried out above them, and the sounds of other riders soon began to buzz around the

43

wheel—nervous laughter, uneasy murmurs, anxious chattering.

David instinctively pulled her back from the safety bar when the car lurched. Vali desperately wished they weren't so near the top of the ride. There was just enough breeze to make the car rock gently back and forth, and she swallowed hard a couple of times against the sick wrenching of her stomach.

David tightened his protective hold on her and gently coaxed her to hide her face against his shoulder. "Dizzy?" he whispered.

She nodded, grateful for his warm closeness. "Is something wrong, do you think?"

"I'm not sure."

She glanced up, and the look of concern etched on his face unsettled her even more. She tried to laugh. "Well, whatever it is, I wish it could have gone wrong when we were a little closer to the ground."

He squeezed her shoulder. "It's all right. Probably just a new operator learning his thing at our expense." With his free hand, he tugged lightly on a russet wave of hair. "Actually, I paid him to keep us up here for a bit. Got you at my mercy now, pretty lady."

She kept her face burrowed into his shoulder, unwilling to move for fear of making the car sway even more. "Don't make fun, David. I don't like this," she appealed to him against the soft cotton of his shirt.

He looked down at her, then rested his chin lightly on the top of her head. "We're all right, princess," he whispered hoarsely into her hair. "Don't you know by now I wouldn't let anything hurt you?"

She looked up at him, feeling her heart turn over when she saw the way he was caressing her with his gaze.

They remained that way for a long moment before a shutter seemed to close in his eyes, and he looked away. He

44

continued to hold her, but now there was nothing more than an awkward silence between them.

Fifteen minutes passed; the voices of riders in the other cars increased in volume, gradually growing more and more agitated. When David tapped her lightly on the shoulder and pointed to the ground, Vali looked, then sighed with relief. The ride operator was helping two young girls out of the car closest to the ground. Then he began to lower the wheel so that each car could empty its passengers. Slowly and methodically every gondola was lowered and emptied until it was David and Vali's turn.

Without knowing why, Vali jerked her hand away when the operator reached out to help her. Saying nothing, the young man raked a thin wisp of blond hair away from his forehead, staring hard at her while David got out.

"Was there a problem?" he asked the operator.

At the sound of David's whisper-voice, the man shot him a questioning look. "No big deal," he muttered. "Slight problem on the axle. Sorry for the delay."

Vali saw David give the man a long, studying look before he turned to lead her outside the ride's gate where Dan and Jennifer were waiting.

" . . . so much for your idea of a nice, leisurely ride, Daniel!" Jennifer was teasing him as Vali and David made their way through the crowd to where the Kaines stood.

Dan wore a sheepish grin. "You have to admit, though, kid, it gave you a good chance to confront your fears."

"That was *not* a confrontation, Daniel," asserted his wife. "That was an *assault.*"

"I think we owe Jennifer a ride of her choice about now," offered David.

Although everyone agreed, somehow, the ride of Jennifer's choice got postponed when the four of them walked by the *Gemini* roller coaster. David mumbled something to Daniel, and both men stopped near the crowd waiting to get on.

Accusing both men of conspiracy, Jennifer turned to Vali. "Are you going on it?"

Vali looked at her, then at David, who grinned and gave her a thumbs-up sign.

"Yes," the singer replied, much to Jennifer's surprise and dismay. "I think I will."

Jennifer sighed. "Then so will I."

Dan looked suspiciously gratified.

Once they arrived at the end of the line, however, Jennifer's resolve began to flag.

"Oh, dear, Daniel . . . . " She attempted a weak laugh. "I am so disappointed . . . but it looks as though I won't be able to do this after all."

"Why not?" he asked her skeptically.

"Well, you see there's one of those signs here that says you have to be *this* tall in order to go on this ride, and I'm afraid I simply won't measure up. I'll just go sit down on a bench and wait."

Dan held her hand with an iron grip. "Nice try, kid. Now, come on."

Jennifer eyed the coaster one more time, swallowed hard, then moved, with all the enthusiasm of a condemned prisoner en route to the execution chamber, to take her place in line.

Feeling a little sick, she stopped to tie her tennis shoe. As she straightened, a rather odd-looking man just off to her right caught her attention. Unnerved by his pale-eyed stare, she suddenly realized that it was Vali who was the focus of his attention, not herself.

She watched him closely. His dark suit and tie were peculiarly out of place in the amusement park, especially on such a warm day. Involuntarily, she shuddered. Something about the man seemed strangely . . . *sinister*. She glanced away for just a second, then returned her gaze to him, disturbed to find his eyes now riveted on her. She turned away from him, willing herself not to look around, but it seemed to her that she could still feel his malevolent stare burning into the back of her head. *Probably just some oddball voyeur*, she thought with distaste.

"What's it look like, Jennifer?" Daniel asked, suddenly breaking into her unsettled thoughts.

She stared up at the coaster, then froze. The double set of twisting, convoluted tracks just ahead of her caused her to utter a soft little sob of denial at the back of her throat.

"Jennifer? What does it looks like?"

She swallowed, then choked, looking slowly from the *Gemini* to her husband. "Like someone's highly detailed, full-scale model of their very worst nightmare," she said thickly. "Daniel . . . you don't want to do this. Trust me."

He rubbed his hands gleefully together. "My kind of coaster."

"Be quiet, Daniel. I'm praying."

"Jennifer—"

"I'm *serious*, Daniel. I *am* praying."

"Boy-oh-boy," he grinned with pleasure. "This is going to be good!"

When the car started up the first incline, Jennifer decided with enormous relief that maybe it wouldn't be so bad after all. She didn't care for the clanking and grinding and lurching. Still, the safety bar seemed secure, and Daniel's large, solid frame next to her gave her what she hoped wasn't a false sense of protection.

It was the first drop that jolted her with the blood-freezing reality of just how wrong she'd been. It was a terrible feeling, a stomach-crushing, mind-exploding feeling.

"*Daniel!*" she screamed. "We're going to fall out!"

"People don't fall out of roller coasters, Jennifer!" he shouted back. "It's got something to do with gravity!"

Gravity! Was that all that was holding them inside this little bitty car? "I *hate* this, Daniel!"

47

"No, you don't!" he yelled with assurance above the din of screaming people and banging clatter. "You're having fun, Jennifer!"

She somehow managed to open her eyes long enough to turn and look at him. With disbelief she saw his upraised arms, the look of pure pleasure on his face, and for goodness' sake, the crazy man was *laughing out loud!*

"It doesn't get any faster, does it, Daniel?" she screamed in terror, unable to hear her own voice as they hugged a death-defying loop.

"Right, honey! It'll get a *lot* faster! You'll love it!" He waved his arms a little more. "Man, this is a *good* one!"

The wind slapped her face. The noise shattered her eardrums. The creaking, clanging metal tracks rose and fell. People screamed. Daniel laughed. Jennifer whimpered.

"You got your hands up, kid?"

"My entire body is paralyzed, Daniel Kaine! The only thing up is my blood pressure!"

"I told you you'd love it, didn't I?"

"Daniel, don't you *hear* me?!"

Then she knew. They were going to plummet off the track. The whole chain of cars was simply going to topple off and go flying into the crowd. She felt the car lean, felt herself being lifted from the seat, then pushed back into place. She looked down, over the side, into the trees; she saw the lake . . . and screamed. Terrorized, she twisted and threw her arms around Daniel's middle, pushed her head under his upraised arm and screamed once more, this time into the hard, safe warmth of his ribs. Her entire body shaking, she silently promised herself that she would never . . . absolutely never . . . let him talk her into anything again. Ever.

The carousel was their final stop before leaving the park, each of them declaring that Jennifer, good sport that she'd been, deserved at least one quiet, *safe* ride.

It was a beautiful carousel with ornate cornices, vivid

panels, elegant chariots and a choice of gallopers, jumpers, and flying horses. The calliope music was loud and happy.

Jennifer and Vali chose two proud looking jumpers, with the men opting for flying horses on the outside.

"Now this is more like it," Jennifer declared as Dan gave her a hand up to her mount before getting on his own somewhat wild-looking stallion. "I love these things. When I was a little girl, I used to ride them over and over again, pretending I was an Indian princess or one of the ladies of King Arthur's court."

Dan grinned at her flight of fancy as he settled onto his horse. Directly in front of them, Vali and David talked in hushed, serious tones, making Jennifer smile at their obvious attraction for each other.

She couldn't help but wonder which man would be best for Vali—David or Graham Alexander. Not that it was any of her business, she reminded herself, but she wasn't sure that she personally approved of either man. Perhaps, though, she was being unfair to the scientist. He obviously cared about the lovely young singer. And while David's interest might be just as obvious, it might *not* be as dependable. Certainly he was a more disturbing kind of man than Alexander appeared to be. Clever and witty and outrageously unconventional one moment, he could turn suddenly quiet and withdrawn the next.

Ah, well, she thought with a tender glance at her husband sitting quietly next to her, not every man could be a Daniel.

She looked around the platform, taking in the horses and the people astride them. Several feet away, a small, red-haired young man with glasses was talking with a dark, lanky youth. She saw the redhead move to start the ride, then stop at something the other boy said. He looked at his wristwatch, then jumped from the platform, leaving his companion to

49

operate the carousel.

Impatient, Jennifer turned to look at the crowd of bystanders off to her right. She drew in a sharp breath of surprise when she caught a glimpse of a familiar face. Standing well behind a number of other people was the same man she'd seen earlier at the *Gemini*, the bald man in the dark business suit.

Her gaze locked with his pale, hard stare. He narrowed his eyes, then glanced from her to Vali before backing out of the crowd and walking off. At the same time, the ride began to move. Jennifer tried to keep track of him as they circled, but he disappeared without her seeing where he went.

She supposed her unease was foolish, but the reappearance of the man troubled her. She was sure she'd never seen him before, but something about him made her feel threatened. More specifically, she realized, he made her feel frightened for Vali.

Abruptly, she attempted to shake off her feelings, determined that nothing was going to spoil this ride. She glanced over at Dan, relishing the sight of his strong, bronzed profile as he sat smilingly at ease on the flying horse. The calliope was playing Strauss; the sun was just beginning to fade below the horizon, and it had been a magical kind of a day.

Jennifer smiled fondly at the memory of the little girl she had been, a little girl who had once ridden this same carousel, her head filled with wonderful, romantic scenarios. Now she had her very own prince, and he was stronger and more handsome than any of the leading men of her schoolgirl dreams. She was in love; she was happy, and life was good.

So caught up in her temporary euphoria was she that the gradual change in the calliope's volume and the slight shift in speed of the rotating platform escaped her notice until Dan, in a sharp voice edged with concern, asked, "What's

50

going on?"

At the same time, she saw Vali turn and dart a worried look at David, who began to cast measuring looks at the frame and inside drive.

The speed was still increasing, the music growing continually louder. Jennifer heard a couple of children begin to cry and saw several people move in closer as they watched. She could hear a growing buzz of alarm among the crowd, and at the same time felt her heart thud loudly, then start to race even faster than the music.

Like a fragment of a bad dream, the platform whirled faster and faster around the circle, horses flying, chariots thumping, the echoing organ music now loud and ugly and distorted.

Jennifer cried out to Dan, who slid off his mount and moved in beside her to wrap a steadying arm around her waist. At the same time, David jumped from his horse and went to Vali, who reached out one hand to clutch at his shoulder.

Raising his free hand to cover Jennifer's white-knuckled grip on the horse rod, Dan asked, "Can you see anything? The ride operator? Where is he?"

They were flying now, faces outside the fence whirling by in a dizzying kaleidoscope of terrified masks.

"I can't see anything!" Jennifer cried hoarsely. "Daniel, don't let go of me!"

In answer, he tightened his grip protectively on her waist.

Suddenly, just when it seemed that the entire carousel would snap and break apart from its inside frame, the music began to slow, then the platform, then Jennifer's heart.

As unexpectedly as it had begun, it was over. David and Vali, whitefaced, turned to look at Jennifer and Dan. The four of them stayed frozen in place for seconds after everything had come to a halt, not speaking, barely breathing.

51

It was Vali who finally broke the strained silence. "Please . . . let's get out of here."

The sound of her voice roused the others into action. Dan helped Jennifer slide from her horse, pulling her safely against him. With the back of his hand, he touched her cheek and felt its dampness. Gently he brushed away her tears.

"You okay, honey?" he whispered into her heavy, windblown hair. "You're not hurt?"

"I'm . . . fine," she said shakily. "I just want to get off, Daniel."

They held each other tightly as she guided him off the platform and away from the ride, walking into the midst of a number of curious, sympathetic bystanders who were murmuring among themselves.

Vali came to stand with them. The three of them waited in tense silence while David and some of the other riders questioned the red-haired carousel operator who apparently had been the one to stop the runaway ride.

When David finally returned, it seemed to Jennifer that his expression was highly skeptical. His face was ashen and taut with controlled anger. "He says he has no idea what happened. Someone sent for him to come to the office; they sent a replacement to operate the ride. By the time he got back here, the other fellow was gone."

Dan, too, lifted his dark brows with a questioning expression but said nothing.

On the way to the exit, their magic day now rudely tarnished, Jennifer's mind raced. She couldn't shake the possibility that there was a connection between the strange looking man in the dark suit and the malfunction of the carousel.

She noticed that David appeared to be half-carrying Vali, who hadn't said a word since leaving the ride. With a worried murmur, she suggested to Dan that they follow the other couple to their car before going to their own.

When they reached David's sleek black Lincoln, the composer turned to them. He dropped his arm away from Vali long enough to shake hands with Daniel, saying, "Thanks for sharing your day with us—I hope it wasn't a total loss for you." His face was granite-hard with tension.

"We enjoyed it," Dan assured him. "Vali? Are you all right?"

David looked at her with concern when she simply hugged her arms a little more tightly to herself without answering Dan.

Before they parted, Jennifer decided to tell the others about the man she'd seen at the *Gemini*, and then again at the carousel.

"He kept staring at Vali," Jennifer continued. "And it was . . . an unpleasant look. Almost a . . . frightening look."

She didn't miss the way David's face paled. "What did the man look like, Jennifer?" His mouth thinned to a hard, tight line, and his whispering voice sounded harsher than usual.

As she described the man with as much detail as she could remember, she saw Vali raise her head and stare at her, wide-eyed. She thought for a moment Vali was going to say something, but the singer remained silent and unmoving.

David, too, had a peculiar, stricken expression on his face. As soon as Jennifer had finished her description, he said a hurried good-bye and helped Vali into the passenger's side of the car. Then he quickly walked around the car and slid into the driver's seat.

It seemed to Jennifer that the enigmatic composer could hardly wait to leave the parking lot. Neither he nor Vali looked back as he drove away.

Shivering, she clung to Dan a little more tightly as they headed toward their own car.

5

Early the next morning, Dan sat on the porch of their cottage in a redwood lawn chair, enjoying the cool air and the sounds coming in off the lake. He could tell by the slapping of the whitecaps that it was choppy this morning, and he found himself wishing he could stand along the shore and watch the seagulls play over the breakers. From somewhere down the beach a dog barked, and beside him, Sunny made a low, answering growl of her own.

Hearing footsteps, Dan sat up a little straighter. Sunny stirred and uttered a perfunctory little bark.

"Morning, Daniel. If you're not the picture of a contented, happy man, I never saw one."

"Hi, David. You're out and about early."

"I like to walk the beach when it's like this. You can almost smell fall in the air."

"Come on up and sit down."

David perched his long, lean frame on the top step of the porch. "I just thought I'd stop and make sure you and Jennifer are both okay. I know your day at Cedar Point wasn't exactly all you'd hoped for."

"We're fine," Dan said easily. "Jennifer's inside getting dressed. Her hair dryer went on the fritz this morning, so we're going to track down a discount store later."

He reached over to rub Sunny's ears. The retriever gradually settled back into her comfortable slouch again, resting her head on both front paws.

"How's Vali?" Dan asked. "Have you talked with her yet this morning?"

"Only by phone. I'm going to stop over in a few minutes before I leave. That's another reason I walked over here, as a

54

matter of fact. I was wondering if I could ask a small favor of you and Jennifer. I hate to keep imposing on you, but . . . . "

Dan made a quick dismissing motion with his hand. "Don't worry about it. Did you say you're leaving?" He took a sip of coffee, then set his cup on the redwood table beside him. "Do you want some coffee? There's plenty."

"No, thanks. I'm sure I'll have more than my limit later on today. I have a meeting with a producer and some other people in Nashville this evening." He fished a stick of gum out of his shirt pocket and tucked it into his mouth. "I'm flying down just for tonight. I plan to be back early tomorrow, but I'm a little concerned about Vali. I was wondering if you and Jennifer would mind giving her a call later today—just to check on her."

"Sure, we'd be glad to. You think she's still upset about yesterday?"

When David didn't answer right away, Dan lifted his chin slightly and frowned. "Jennifer was afraid she might have made things worse by telling us about the man she saw at the rides."

"Vali isn't . . . very strong, Daniel," the composer said slowly. "Emotionally, I mean. She's had some problems that way."

"I thought maybe that was all behind her. I heard she had a real bad time after Paul Alexander's death, but that was three years ago."

He heard the frustration in David's deep sigh as he shifted restlessly on the step. "Most of the time she seems all right. But it doesn't take much to upset her. She was badly frightened last night. I couldn't get her to talk to me at all until this morning. Now she's trying to laugh it off, but I'm just a little uneasy about her being alone today."

"Vali said Graham was out of town, too. Is he still gone?"

"Yes," David rasped shortly. "He won't be back until some time tomorrow."

"Well, we'll be happy to check on her. Jennifer will be glad for a chance to say hello."

"Thanks, Dan—I really appreciate it." He paused, then said, "Your Jennifer is a real special lady."

Dan smiled. "Yes, she surely is."

"Did you know each other for a long time before you got married?"

"Not really. I hired her as my exec at the radio station around the first of the year and fell head over heels in love with her—the same day, I think." He hesitated, then asked, "What about you, David? Do you have a girl? Someone special in your life?"

The musician didn't answer for a moment. When he did, his whisper-voice was softer than ever. "Not . . . exactly." After a slight pause, he added, "Just a wish."

"Vali?"

"It's that obvious?"

"Jennifer is always on the lookout for romance. She's hard to fool." Dan couldn't stop a smile at the thought of his wife's quick mind and inquisitive nature.

"Well . . . the competition is pretty tough, I'm afraid."

"Graham Alexander?"

"He's a rather formidable opponent."

"They're not engaged, are they? Jennifer said she didn't notice Vali wearing a ring."

"No, not yet. But Graham is giving it his best shot."

Dan shrugged and lifted his eyebrows. "Until she's wearing a ring, you've got a chance."

"Not much of one, I'm afraid." David sounded discouraged as he went on to explain. "Graham has a definite edge on me. You see, Vali feels enormously indebted to him."

Dan looked surprised. "Why?"

"You know that Graham is Paul Alexander's twin?"

Dan nodded.

"Well, after his brother died, Graham more or less made himself responsible for Vali's welfare. You see, Vali had a complete breakdown after Paul died."

Dan heard him get up and step down off the porch.

"All I know is what I've been told by others," he continued, "but it's common knowledge that she fell apart emotionally. She wouldn't sing; she wouldn't eat, wouldn't see anyone— wouldn't even go out of the house, I understand."

"She's obviously better." Dan reached for his coffee cup, then felt for the pot to pour himself a refill.

"Oh, yes, she definitely is," David quickly agreed. "Though I'd like to see her a lot . . . stronger. More secure about herself, at least. At any rate," he continued, "she attributes her present . . . well-being . . . to Graham."

Puzzled, Dan asked, "Why is that?"

The composer hesitated for a long moment. "Apparently Graham and his mother brought Vali up here, after her . . . breakdown. They saw to it that she got excellent care in a local sanitarium for several months. After that, I believe she lived with Leda—that's Graham's mother—for a few weeks until she moved into her own place here on the beach. They seem to have appointed themselves her guardians— not in the legal sense, but certainly in every other way. Graham in particular keeps a very watchful, protective eye on Vali."

Dan could hear an undercurrent of resentment in David's words. "It sounds as if he might have been fond of her when she was still engaged to his brother," he said thoughtfully.

"No, that's the odd thing," David replied. "From what Vali's told me, she and Graham barely knew one another until after the airplane crash. She and Leda had spent some time together, and I think they got close right from the beginning. But that wasn't the case with her and Graham. Anyway, that all changed after Paul died. Now, she seems to feel an extraordinary sense of gratitude toward the man. In fact—" he hesitated for an instant—"I suppose this will sound like nothing more than jealousy, but I get the feeling that Graham Alexander has fostered a kind of . . . unhealthy dependency in Vali."

"A dependency on him, you mean."

"Yes. I think he has her convinced that she can't function without him, that she's . . . incompetent . . . on her own."

Dan had his doubts about the musician's observation, but simply asked, "Why would someone with Vali Tremayne's talent and reputation get involved in a relationship like that?"

"It's just a hunch, but I think Graham discovered Vali's weakness and capitalized on it. You see, she has this incredibly distorted sense of her own worth. At some time in her life, her self-image was virtually destroyed—or maybe it never developed. As illogical as it may seem, considering who she is—and how special she is—Vali has a total lack of self-confidence. I think she's probably the most insecure person I've ever known."

Dan's frown deepened as he distractedly ran his thumb around the rim of his cup. "Yet she's a Christian."

"She was also an orphan," David replied. "Apparently she was tossed around from one foster home to another for years. I'm convinced that's at the heart of her problems. Vali loves the Lord with all her heart, and in her own way she has a close walk with Him. But she has no understanding whatever, no real acceptance, of herself." He paused, then added, "I imagine we both know Christians who have been spiritually weakened because they're unable to either understand or accept their own worth in the Lord's eyes. With Vali, I'm afraid it's become a critical emotional problem."

Dan was quiet for a long time, then said, "She must trust you a great deal to confide in you as she has."

David hesitated before answering. "A lot of what I know I learned from other people," he admitted. "But, yes, she *has* shared some things about her past with me. The rest . . well, I care so much about her, I think I often just . . . sense her feelings."

"Does she know you're in love with her?" Dan asked gently.

"I'm afraid I haven't done very well at hiding it."

"Well—" Dan stroked one side of his jaw thoughtfully— "maybe you're just what she needs to break this . . . *dependency* . . . on Graham Alexander."

"Naturally, I'd like to think so," David grated with his small, voiceless laugh. "But I don't have a whole lot of time left, I'm afraid."

"What do you mean?"

"The agreement was that Vali and I would work together for a few weeks, then she'd make a decision as to whether or not she's actually going to return to her career. Her agent, a former producer—a number of people, in fact—are counting on me to coax her back into performing again. But in the meantime, I have recording commitments of my own to honor, and my time is running out. Soon, I'll have to go back to Nashville to stay."

"But you could still see her—"

"Once I leave here, Dan, my chance is over. If I can't convince Vali to pick up the pieces of her career—and to leave Graham Alexander in the wings—while I'm cloistered with her for hours every day, I certainly can't hope to do it when I'm hundreds of miles away from her. No. If I leave here and Vali decides to stay, Graham wins."

"That almost sounds like a war," Dan said mildly.

The composer was silent for a long time. Dan could hear the strain in his whisper-voice when he replied, "In a way, Daniel, it is. But I happen to believe it's a war worth fighting."

59

"In a war, David, someone always gets hurt. And someone always loses."

"Yes, I know," the musician whispered. "But I can promise you this, Daniel, whether I win or lose, I intend to make sure that Vali isn't the one who gets hurt."

After the composer had walked away, Dan bent forward in his chair and propped his elbows on his knees, then balanced his chin on top of his folded hands. He ran through everything David had told him, puzzling as he had more than once, over his conflicting impressions of the man.

Being blind made it difficult to "read" another person, although he'd become reasonably adept at gauging the emotional barometers of those around him. It suddenly occurred to him, however, that even if he were to see David's face, he quite possibly wouldn't know any more about the enigmatic musician than he already did. A deepseated but growing doubt about the man made Dan wonder whether anyone really saw the true face of David Nathan Keye.

6

The man shifted his tall frame inside the phone booth, keeping one eye on the highway a few feet away.

"That fiasco at Cedar Point was incredibly stupid! What in the world possessed you? And to go yourself—"

The voice on the other end of the phone sighed with exaggerated patience. "Calm yourself. Didn't I explain that we were simply going to . . . assist you with your plan? It was all quite safe."

"It was foolish, not safe!" the man snarled. "The only thing you accomplished was to make the Kaine woman suspicious."

"What do you mean?" The voice hardened.

"She *saw* you, that's what I mean. She saw you *twice*, as a matter of fact."

"How do you know?"

"She made a point of describing you. What's more, Vali couldn't talk about anything else when I called her this morning. She's more on edge now than ever."

"Then the day was a success. You need her disoriented, do you not?"

"I don't need her watching her shadow! And I most certainly don't need that blind snoop and his wife nosing around to find out what's going on!"

"You're allowing your anxiety to distract you from the fact that all this is working to our advantage."

The man pulled at his shirt collar. "Listen to me. I know what I'm doing. If you'll just stay out of it and give me the time I need, I can tie up all the loose ends permanently."

The voice sighed again. "Time is becoming of extreme importance, my friend. We've been patient with your infatuation with the Tremayne woman and your insistence that you can effectively silence her. But the truth is—"

"I told you—"

"*The truth is*," the voice interrupted with an icy note of warning, "that you're not much farther along with your plan today than you were when we started. Now, we both know there's a good possibility that the lady could put us—and a number of other people, important people—behind bars for the rest of our natural lives. In addition," he pressed on in an even, cold tone, ignoring the attempt of the other man to object, "the unfortunate return of her memory of certain events could prove disastrous to a project it has taken years to implement. That cannot be allowed. The Tremayne woman is to be neutralized. Your way, if you can accomplish it within five more days." He paused, drew a deep breath, and added quietly, "*Our* way, if not. Is that clear?"

"Perfectly clear," the man grated resentfully.

"And don't give the other couple—the *Kaines*, is it?—a second thought. If they should turn out to be a problem or complicate our plans in any way, they're entirely expendable. We'll take care of them."

7

The evening was summertime warm, the lake calm, the breeze gentle. Dan and Jennifer strolled leisurely along the beach, his right arm resting lightly around her shoulders, his other hand firmly gripping Sunny's harness. They walked in contented silence, Jennifer watching the sun set, Daniel smiling softly to himself as he allowed his thoughts free rein.

He knew it would surprise most people to learn that he counted himself a peaceful, happy man. The reason for his peace was his overflowing love for a Lord who continually amazed him with His goodness and His faithfulness. The reason for his happiness was the woman walking closely at his side.

In his usual manner, he prayed as he walked, sometimes silently, sometimes in a soft murmur, unaware of the infinitely tender attention of his wife.

How she had changed his life . . . sweetened it, enriched it, given it a meaning and an ongoing joy he wouldn't have dared to hope for until they met.

His smile abruptly faded as an uninvited memory surfaced, bringing with it a sudden, wrenching pain. All too clearly, he remembered another evening walk along a beach.

It hadn't been a happy time, that summer he'd spent in Florida only months after the automobile accident that had blinded him. In truth, it had been one of the most difficult times of his life, a time when he was trying to fight his way through the seemingly endless and insurmountable problems of his blindness. Gabe Denton, his closest friend, had insisted that Dan put the station under temporary management and get away—away from home, from work, and from painful memories. Dan had reluctantly given in to Gabe's urging, and they spent two months in a rented house on a private beach.

Loneliness had tormented him like a viper that summer evening, striking at him, stabbing at him along with discouragement and fear ... the fear that he would spend the rest of his life, not only without sight, but without warmth, without love, without hope ... that he would grow old alone, never knowing the companionship or joy of having a wife and a family. He and Gabe had walked for hours in silence along the deserted beach, neither of them able to voice each other's private dread. For one brief, desolate moment, Dan had felt an almost overwhelming urge to simply walk into the sea and let it take him.

Even years after he finally made peace with his Lord about the blindness, the awful loneliness had still lingered, sometimes threatening to break him. Too many times he experienced the unsighted person's dilemma of feeling alone in the midst of a crowd, even among his own family— cut off, isolated, a solitary man in a lonely world.

But then ... then Jennifer had come sweeping into his life, into his heart. Jennifer, his sweet, gate-crashing rebel, with her wild, wonderful mane of hair that smelled like sunshine and her honey-flowing voice that warmed his soul ... Jennifer, with the laugh that shattered his doubts, the touch that melted his senses, and the love that conquered his fears and set him free—free to love her. *Oh, my Lord ... my loving, gracious Lord, how can I ever, ever thank you enough for her?*

Hearing his soft praise, Jennifer smiled up at his profile. "What are you thinking about, Daniel?"

"Just counting my blessings, darlin' ... again," he said

with the love-touched smile that was reserved for her alone.

She wrapped her arm around his waist and hugged him tightly. "We have a bunch of them to count, don't we, Daniel?"

"Indeed we do, love. Indeed we do."

"Do you ever feel . . . guilty? Because we're so happy and other people aren't?"

"No," he said truthfully. "Just extremely grateful. What prompted that question, darlin'?"

"Oh, I don't know." She poked at a mound of sand with the toes of her bare foot. "When I see someone like Vali Tremayne, I feel almost ashamed that I can be so happy, when she's so . . . miserable."

Dan stopped walking. "Do you really think she's that unhappy?"

"Yes," Jennifer replied without hesitation. "I think she's *terribly* unhappy, Daniel. And I wish there were something we could do about it."

"I know, honey," he said quietly, squeezing her shoulder. "But I'm afraid all we can do right now is what David asked us to do. Why don't we walk over to her cottage and make sure she's okay?"

As Vali neared the sea wall a few feet from her cottage, she called the cat one more time, then turned to leave the beach and go back inside.

Seeing Dan and Jennifer approaching from the other direction, she stopped, waved to them, and waited to say hello.

Her pleased smile was genuine; she liked Jennifer Kaine more than any other woman she'd ever met, except for Leda, perhaps. To her surprise, Jennifer seemed to like *her*, also.

Vali had never had a close woman friend, even in college. She'd been far too shy back then to make any gesture of friendship on her own. Later, after she and Paul had become successful as a team in the Christian music industry, she hadn't felt the need for anyone in her life except him. Paul had often encouraged her to make friends with some of the other young women they met in their professions, but Vali had never been comfortable in initiating any kind of relationship.

After Paul's death, she hadn't wanted anyone. Leda had been there, of course, and Vali owed the older woman a great deal. But she was more a mother figure than a friend, more a source of strength than someone to share with on a mutual level.

Now, as she saw the open friendliness on Jennifer's face, she wished there could be more time to get to know her—and Daniel, too. They made her feel wanted and they made her feel . . . likable. For the most part, she was unacquainted with both feelings.

"Hi, Vali!" Jennifer called warmly. "You going for a walk, too?"

"I've already been. Actually, I've been trying to find my runaway cat again."

Daniel laughed. "Does Trouble ever stay home where she belongs?"

"Not very often, I'm afraid. At least, I seem to spend an awful lot of time trying to track her down."

"Are you worried about her?" Jennifer asked.

"Oh, no. She'll show up before long, once she realizes it's past dinnertime. You two look like you got some sun today," she observed, glancing from Jennifer to Dan.

"And a few new freckles," Jennifer said, rubbing the tip of her nose. "We spent most of the day on the beach. Dan, of course, just keeps turning darker and darker, but I feel a little pink in places."

"It was a good day to get a burn," Vali said, "but I hope it doesn't stay this warm all night. My air conditioner isn't working right, and I haven't been able to get a repairman yet this week."

After a few more minutes of small talk, they parted. Dan and Jennifer walked on down the beach as Vali neared the porch of her cottage.

Calling Trouble one more time before giving up, Vali went inside, closing the front door behind her. She'd left a table lamp on before going on her search, and she now walked over to the hanging lamp behind the studio piano and turned it on, too.

As always, Vali had drawn the drapes long before dark. She hated darkness; even after she went to bed she always left a lamp burning in the cottage. Paul had once helped her trace this aversion, which she knew bordered on nycto-phobia, to one of the many foster "mothers" in her past. This particular caretaker had often indulged her penchant for discipline by locking Vali in a small, dark and mildewy basement under the kitchen when her behavior wasn't acceptable. Frequently, Vali had been made to stay there, alone and terrified, throughout an entire night.

She wondered if her fear of the dark had anything to do with the intensity of compassion she had felt for Daniel Kaine when she first realized he was blind. Crossing the room to the couch, she shuddered at the thought of what Daniel had to endure every day of his life.

She reached for the newspaper on the table beside the couch, then decided to fix a cup of tea before settling in for the evening. On her way through the small dinette that separated the living room from the kitchen, Vali stooped to pick up one of Trouble's yarn balls. As she straightened, she caught a glimpse of something not quite right in the direction of the kitchen. Without moving, she held her breath, staring into the gaping blackness of the open back door. She was positive the door had been closed and locked before she left the cottage for her walk.

Not making a sound, she continued to stare at the open door. She listened but heard nothing; waited but saw nothing.

The skin on her forearms tightened as she fought to control her fear. Someone had been in her cottage. Someone had come inside her home, boldly leaving the door open behind him.

Where was he now?

A sudden, involuntary image flashed through her mind, rocking her with startled fear. *The man at the ferris wheel.* The man Jennifer had seen again at the carousel. The man with the cold, malevolent eyes. She shook her head to banish his face. What had made her think of him?

Had he been the one watching her cottage earlier in the summer? She tensed even more, remembering the faceless figure who had stood outside in the darkness several weeks ago, never revealing himself, never approaching her. Simply . . . watching.

What if he were still inside the cottage?

Don't panic. Breathe . . . take a deep breath . . . listen.

Slowly a gradual sensation of relief settled over her, a feeling that, whoever might have been inside, he was no longer in the cottage. She was alone now, she was sure of it.

She would shut the door. She moved to steady herself by bracing one hand on the lacquered dinette table. Her eyes finally focused enough to make out shadowed images around her, and stiffly, carefully, she forced herself to take one tentative step at a time until she was standing in the middle of the kitchen.

Should she turn on the light? She desperately wanted to, wanted to flood the room with its brightness, but something made her wait.

She stared at the door for a full minute or more before she was able to will herself forward. Finally she hurled herself at it, grabbing onto it with both hands, slamming it shut and locking it with one frenzied motion.

Shaking violently, she continued to press herself, face forward, against the door, pushing her fingers hard against the wood, breathing in hurried, shallow gulps.

Now what? She turned around, slowly, reluctantly. Finally her heartbeat slowed a little, and she was able to grab a couple of normal breaths.

She knew she had to search the cottage. *If only David hadn't gone away . . . or if Graham were here.*

Startled by the realization that she'd thought of David first, she felt guilty and quickly turned her thoughts away from him. *Graham . . . it's Graham I need; Graham I want, not David.*

But Graham wasn't here; he was still in Cleveland. And David had gone to Nashville. *She had to do something . . . she had to move.* Taking one more deep breath, she fumbled along the wall for the light switch, flipped it, and waited.

There was no sound, no movement. Nothing.

She had to search the rest of the cottage. She knew the living room was safe, having just come from there. That left only her bedroom and the small bath.

She looked around, moved to open the silverware drawer, and took out a knife, uneasily aware of the fact that it could be used on her by an intruder lurking somewhere in the darkness. She almost replaced it, then decided to keep it.

She left the kitchen and crossed the narrow hallway to her bedroom, stopping just outside the open doorway.

The room was dark, shadowed, oppressively quiet. She took one step, heard something, backed off, and waited.

Silence.

Once again she took a small step into the room, then another. Unable to stand the darkness any longer, she felt her way toward the night table by the bed and with trembling fingers switched on the lamp, casting a soft glow of light into the room.

Reassured by the lively garden colors and splashes of floral prints scattered throughout the room, Vali swallowed against the sour taste of fear in her mouth and lifted her chin determinedly.

She took her time looking around the room, growing more and more relieved at its apparent normalcy. Walking around the bed, she began to pace the length and width of the room, a growing calm now gradually easing the tense set of her features.

Then she heard the noise again. It was coming from the closet.

She stared with fear-widened eyes at the closed door.

A soft thud, then another. Her right hand went up to her mouth, clenched into a tight, defensive fist.

Out of the corner of her eye she saw the open bedroom door, thought about bolting from the room, then wondered if there was safety anywhere else in the cottage.

There was someone in the closet.

What if she hadn't heard the noise until later? She would have come into the room, undressed for her shower, gone into the adjoining bathroom, and then . . .

Get out of the room!

But what was he waiting for? He'd had any number of opportunities to grab her by now.

What did he want?

She suddenly remembered the knife in her hand. She glanced down at it, then raised her eyes to the door of the closet.

She began to walk. Carefully, softly, slowly.

She stopped once, looked down again at the knife, then went on.

Something scraped at the door, louder now, more insistent.

He was baiting her, teasing her, playing games with her.

She covered the brass knob with her left hand, paused, then yanked it as hard as she could. The door flew open, slamming all the way against the wall with a loud thud.

Vali raised the knife, staring into the blackness of the closet, squinting among her hanging wardrobe, up to the shelves, then down at the floor.

Something lunged at her, hit her foot, and screeched.

Vali screamed. Then screamed again, staring with horror, then disbelief, at the small gray and white ball of fur now wrapping itself eagerly around her ankles, weaving in and out, and humming in a low, welcoming purr.

"*Trouble!*"

The knife fell from her hand, clattering onto the wooden floor. The cat jumped, darted an accusing look at her owner, then raced from the room, scurrying across the living room and under the piano bench.

Vali didn't know whether to laugh, cry, or catch the cat and shake it. Relief—and a self-conscious sense of humiliation—cascaded over her in waves as she stood shaking, as much now from the weakness of knowing how foolish she'd been as from the aftermath of fear.

"You bad, bad kitten!" she scolded, walking into the living room and glaring down between the bench and the piano, where Trouble sat huddled, watching and apparently waiting to see what Vali was going to do.

"So *you're* my intruder!" she accused, too relieved to be angry. She was positive now that she'd simply left the back door unlocked. One of Trouble's favorite tricks was to insert a paw in the opening underneath a door, then pry and push at it until it opened. Obviously, the cat had played with the

71

unlocked door until she'd opened it and let herself in, leaving the door open behind her.

With a rueful smile, Vali thought about the other times the kitten had maneuvered herself into a room or a closet using the same method.

But would the cat have shut the closet door behind her, once she'd gone inside? She moistened her lips and glanced back toward the bedroom. It was possible, she reassured herself. Trouble was always doing things other cats never seemed to think of. Shutting a closet door was . . . well . . . certainly it was possible.

She shook her head at her skittishness, then went to the couch and sat down, willing the last of her nervousness to ebb and dissolve.

No longer in the mood to read, she was reaching for the TV's remote control when the phone on the lamp table beside the couch shrilled.

Still jumpy, Vali flinched, stared at the phone for a moment, then lifted the receiver. Eager for a friendly voice, she expected to hear Leda Alexander's strident, no-nonsense greeting. Graham's mother called every evening, usually about this time.

"You should be more careful about locking your doors, Vali."

The voice was a harsh, unpleasant whisper. Stunned, Vali jerked the receiver away from her ear, staring at it as though it were a snake about to strike.

It was a full minute before she could bring herself to put the receiver to her ear again.

"Don't worry about it, Vali . . . I'm going to be looking after you tonight . . . all night . . . . Soon I'll be right there with you."

Frozen, Vali was unable to speak.

" . . . Be sure to keep your doors locked until I get there, Vali . . . but don't worry about waiting up for me . . . I'll let

72

myself in . . . just as I did while you were walking on the beach . . . . Incidentally, Vali—did you ever find that naughty cat of yours?"

She slammed down the receiver with a loud bang, releasing it with shaking hands as if it had seared her skin.

No sooner was the connection broken than the phone began to ring again.

She covered her ears with her hands, staring at the phone through terrified eyes.

Let it ring . . . don't pick it up.

It rang for a full two minutes before it stopped, leaving an ominous silence in the cottage.

She glanced around the room, then bolted to the large picture window. It was locked, and the drapes were completely closed. She peered out from one side behind the drapes, seeing nothing.

Suddenly she drew back with a frightened gasp, remembering the bedroom window she'd left open earlier because of the broken air conditioner.

While she was racing from the living room into the bedroom, the telephone started ringing again.

Stop it! Stop doing this to me!

Frantically, her hand trembling, she cranked the small casement window shut and locked it.

The phone was still ringing.

Her back to the wall by the window, she stood staring blankly through the open doorway, across the hall into the living room.

Help me . . . help me, Lord . . . make it stop . . . make him stop doing this to me . . . you know how afraid I am, Lord . . . please make him stop . . . .

Silence again. She pried herself away from the wall and went to check the kitchen window, then the door again, even though she'd locked it only moments earlier.

She had to think. She stood in the middle of the kitchen, then remembered the small jalousie window in the bathroom and hurried back across the hall to check it.

The cat was now behind her, curious and wanting to play. Vali screamed at it, sending it fleeing back to the living room.

The front door . . . are you sure you locked it, too?

She went to check and found both the lockset and the dead bolt secure.

There. No one could get in now. There was no way.

Unless they wanted in badly enough to break a window.

Should she turn out all the lights, so no movement could be seen from outside? No. He might think she'd gone to bed. She wanted him to know she was awake and watching. Besides, she couldn't spend the rest of the night in the dark, she'd go crazy.

She had to call the police. Now.

The jangle of the telephone made every muscle in her body go into spasms again.

She yanked the receiver off the hook and screamed into it. "*Stop it!*" Softer, she said again, "Stop this . . . please."

"*I hope you found your naughty kitten, Vali. I put her in the closet for you, so she couldn't run away again. You have pretty things in your closet, Vali. I especially like the pink silk dress. Is it real silk, Vali?*"

Sobbing, she threw the receiver at the table.

That was when the lights went out.

She panicked, cried out hysterically, then dropped to the floor, crouching in a terrified huddle against the back of the couch. Her eyes were wild, her breathing labored in the inky darkness.

Trouble came padding noiselessly over to where she was crouched, nuzzling Vali's clenched hands and purring softly as she pressed her small head into her owner's lap.

74

Vali glanced down at the cat with vacant eyes, seeing nothing.

Call someone while you still can . . . call the police.

She wouldn't be able to see the number in the dark . . . .

Try to find it . . . call the Kaines . . . call Leda.

That's what she'd do. She knew Leda's number by heart. She'd call her and Leda would send the police.

She began to crawl around the back, then the side of the couch. When she reached the table, she got to her feet and fumbled for the receiver. It was dangling over the side of the table. She retrieved it with a clammy, shaking hand.

The phone was dead. Somehow, in the few minutes since the last call—how long had it been?—he had disconnected her phone—or had she done it herself by throwing the receiver?

Now she was completely cut off from any kind of help. She was alone. In the dark.

Irrationally, she picked up the telephone, yanked it out of the wall connection, and hurled it across the room.

Something moved outside. Close to the wall of the cottage. It cracked, like a branch snapping. Then stopped.

Vali's wild gaze turned in the direction of the sound, toward the wall just across from where she was standing.

The knife . . . what had she done with the knife . . .

Something began to scrape softly at the screened window on the wall, slowly, then faster, rougher, louder. He began to pound then, thumping on the outside with hard, even thuds. Soon the pounding became louder, frenzied, louder and louder until the very walls seemed to shake.

Vali backed away, her eyes riveted on the wall where the pounding was coming from. She slid slowly down the wall, her hands covering her ears, her mouth opening and closing in soft little cries of appeal.

The pounding went on and on . . . she could barely hear it

with her ears tightly covered, but she could feel the vibration of it, her body shaking with every thud.

Past screaming, she lay weakly against the wall and waited. *Please help me . . . Father . . .*

Suddenly the banging on the wall became a banging on the door . . . a crashing, wood-splitting sound.

A man's voice, fierce and demanding, shouted at her, "Vali! Open the door! Vali!"

8

Jennifer set a cup of hot tea on the table in front of Vali, then lightly touched her shoulder. "Drink this, Vali," she urged softly. "Is there anything else I can get for you?"

Vali shook her head. She lifted the cup with a trembling hand, spilling some of the tea before it reached her lips.

Dan drew back a chair and sat down across from her, saying nothing. The drumbeat of his fingers on the tabletop was the only sound in the compact kitchen. Everyone seemed to be making an effort to keep things quiet for Vali's sake. Jennifer had a brief, unpleasant sensation of the stillness of a house after a death. It was as if an ordinary level of noise would be intolerable, given the present extra-ordinary circumstances.

Graham Alexander stood directly behind Vali, his hands resting protectively on her shoulders. His mother had drawn a chair up next to Vali and was now studying the younger woman's face with maternal concern, absently patting her hand from time to time in a reassuring gesture.

Leda Alexander had been a surprise to Jennifer. The Greek-born novelist looked to be in her early fifties; she was short and attractive, with dark hair and olive-toned skin. Instead of the cosmopolitan sophisticate Jennifer had expected, the internationally acclaimed novelist was slightly overweight, plainly dressed, and gave off an unaffected air of common sense and comfort. Her warm smile and direct manner immediately put Jennifer at ease; she decided without hesitation that Graham's mother would be far easier to like than her son.

Jennifer had to admit, however, that Graham's tone sounded genuine enough when he said, "We're deeply indebted to you and your wife, Mr. Kaine. If you hadn't been worried enough to come over here last night and check on Vali, there's no telling what might have happened."

Dan quickly dismissed the man's gratitude with a slight shake of his head, directing his reply to Vali. "I'm just sorry I broke down your door, Vali. We were almost positive you were here, and when you didn't answer the phone, we had the operator check your line."

"That's when we got concerned—" Jennifer explained in a rush of words—"because she said your line was out of order. When we got over here and you didn't come to the door, I really got scared. And when Daniel started pounding on your door and we heard you scream—well, we didn't know what to do. We were afraid someone was inside with you. Daniel finally decided to break in."

"And we're so grateful he did," Leda Alexander said. "Vali must have been beside herself by then."

"Vali . . . dear, what I don't understand is why you simply didn't answer the door when the Kaines arrived," Graham said with a small frown, noticeably tightening his grasp on the singer's narrow shoulders.

Jennifer saw Vali tense even more. Her voice sounded weak and strained when she answered him. "I told you, Graham, I . . . panicked."

Graham nodded his head knowingly, darting an "I-told-you-so" glance at his mother.

Leda, however, seemed unaware of her son's pointed look. "Of course, you were, darling. Anyone would have been terrified by what you went through."

Graham sounded less convinced. "But surely you recognized Mr. Kaine's—*Daniel's*—voice, dear."

Vali darted an embarrassed glance at Dan and Jennifer. "I should have . . . I know . . . but I was so frightened, Graham," she said, turning to look up at him.

He nodded with no apparent conviction, touching her

gently on top of her head as though she were an unreliable child. "It's all right, dear. We understand."

Jennifer was surprised to see anger spark in Vali's eyes. "No, I don't think you do, Graham! You weren't there—you couldn't possibly know what it was like for me!"

The scientist lifted a disapproving eyebrow but said nothing.

"I didn't *imagine* it, Graham!"

"Vali," Graham's mother quickly interrupted, "Graham knows it happened just as you told us. He's just concerned for you, darling, that's all. Now—" she squeezed Vali's hand and smiled at her—"I want you to throw some things in your overnighter. You can spend a few days with me until the police get this awful thing straightened out."

Vali looked at Leda uncertainly. "I don't know, Leda . . . I don't think—"

"Mother's right, Vali," Graham said firmly. "You can't possibly stay here until we get your door repaired and the police take care of—this other business."

"But, Graham, I don't want—"

"Vali? You in here?"

It was David. Without waiting for a reply, he walked inside, coming to stand at the doorway of the kitchen.

He stopped just over the threshold of the room, his gray, heavy-lidded eyes sweeping each person there for an instant before settling on Vali. In one hand he held a bouquet wrapped in green floral paper; a few buds of crimson roses peeped out the top.

"Well, I was about to wish you a happy birthday, princess, but it looks as if the party's already begun. What happened to the front door?"

With surprise, Jennifer turned to stare at Vali. "Today is your birthday, Vali? And you haven't said a word!"

David walked the rest of the way in. He was wearing sheeting pants and a regatta shirt. His sunglasses were

79

perched on top of his head. Jennifer thought he looked slightly rumpled and tired.

He walked over to Vali and made a low bow and a wide, sweeping motion with the bouquet. "Happy birthday, princess," he said, handing her the roses.

Jennifer looked from David to Graham Alexander. She wasn't too surprised to see the scientist's handsome features tighten into an unpleasant, frigid mask.

David flicked an indifferent glance at Graham before warmly greeting Leda. He then returned his attention to Vali, who gave him a brief, hesitant smile. "Thank you, David," she said softly, pushing her chair back so she could stand. "I'll put them in water."

Leda laid a restraining hand on Vali's arm. "You stay put, darling. I'll do it." She got up, took the roses, and started across the room, then stopped for a moment to give David a searching look. "Vali had some trouble last night. She's awfully upset."

David quickly squatted down beside Vali's chair. "What kind of trouble, princess? What happened?"

Before Vali could answer, Graham's hands clasped her shoulders even more firmly. "I don't think it's a good idea for Vali to go through all the details again," he said evenly. "It will only make it more difficult for her."

Ignoring him, David covered Vali's hand with his own and asked again, "Vali?"

She tipped her head to glance up at Graham before turning her gaze to David. It seemed to Jennifer that Vali's desire to confide in the composer was obvious. "Some-one . . . was in the cottage last night."

"*What?*" He stiffened. "Who? What happened?" he asked grimly, searching Vali's eyes.

She described to him then, in her soft, faltering voice, the events of the night before. When she was done, David gently released her hand and stood.

80

"You called the police?" David asked, looking at Graham.

The scientist bristled. "Of course, we called the police," he answered caustically. "They've already been here. When you arrived, we were about to help Vali get some of her things packed so she can spend a few days with Mother."

David looked from Graham to Vali. "Is that what you want to do, princess?"

Vali's voice was hesitant and tremulous; she didn't meet David's gaze but stared woodenly down at her lap. As she spoke, she hugged her arms tightly against her body. "I . . . I have to get my door repaired. I can't stay here until it's fixed."

David nodded and once again dropped down beside her. "Is there anything I can do, princess? Any way I can help?"

Jennifer's throat tightened at the way the composer was studying Vali's face. *He adores her,* she thought with certainty. *He truly does love her.*

The thought gave her no satisfaction. She still felt a sense of unease about the man, in spite of his undeniable charm and apparent devotion to Vali. It puzzled her, how she could like him—and she did—but at the same time not completely trust him.

It occurred to her that Vali might be better off without *either* of the two men who were trying to claim her affection. David made her uncomfortable; she couldn't quite shake the feeling he was hiding something. And Graham—*face it, Jennifer . . . you just don't like the man.* Not a very Christian sentiment, but there it was. She thought him cold, condescending, and overbearing.

His frosty, precise tone abruptly penetrated her thoughts. "Vali said you were out of town, David. When, exactly, did you return?"

David glanced up at him, studying his face for a long

moment before he finally answered. "I was in Nashville, Graham. And I returned just this morning." He got to his feet, his eyes glinting with challenge. "Why do you ask?"

Graham examined the musician with a cold, thorough stare. "The man who called Vali last night spoke in what she described as a . . . hoarse whisper."

The underlying accusation hung tensely between them. No one spoke as the two men silently glared at each other. David's face was ashen, but he continued to meet Graham's look with a steady gaze of his own. "A common enough method of disguising your voice, I believe, Graham," he said. "One that's used rather frequently, I imagine."

Something flared in the scientist's eyes, then subsided. He shrugged, and the moment was broken.

"Vali," he said solicitously, moving from behind her chair to interpose himself between her and David, "let Mother help you pack now. We need to get you settled so you can rest. I'll see to it that your door is repaired as soon as possible."

"And the phone, too," Vali reminded him.

"The phone?" David looked questioningly from Vali to Graham.

"The line was cut," Graham answered curtly.

David's face blanched, but he remained silent.

"Vali, darling," Leda said from where she was standing at the kitchen counter, "this was supposed to be a surprise, but I'm going to tell you now because there's no way I can keep it a secret all afternoon if you go home with me. Besides, I think you'll want your new friends to know."

She smiled at Dan and Jennifer, then, in answer to Vali's puzzled expression, explained, "I had planned a small party for this evening—to celebrate your birthday."

"Oh, Leda—I don't want . . ."

"I knew you wouldn't *want*—" Leda waved away her objection. "That's why it was going to be a surprise. Just us, and Graham and David, of course. And Jeff Daly."

Graham gave her a clearly disapproving look and said distastefully, "You're still seeing him?"

His mother reddened, then raised her chin and countered, "As often as possible, Graham."

He twisted his mouth into an unpleasant scowl, but said nothing.

"Anyway," Leda continued, "now that you know, Vali, I thought you'd like Daniel and Jennifer to come, too." She smiled at Jennifer and added, "If you can, that is."

Jennifer glanced at Dan, who seemed to sense her question. "It's up to you, honey," he said.

"We wouldn't want to intrude on a family evening," Jennifer said hesitantly.

"Oh, but you wouldn't be," Leda insisted. "We'd love to have you."

"Please, Jennifer," Vali added. "I'd really like for you and Daniel to come."

"Mother, the Kaines are on their honeymoon, I believe," Graham said stiffly. "We're making it difficult for them to refuse, but I hardly think they'd be interested in a family dinner."

Jennifer was surprised when Daniel settled the issue by interjecting firmly, "We'll be there." Rising from his chair, he added, "But I think we'd better be going now."

Jennifer got up and, after studying Vali's forlorn expression for a moment, walked over and impulsively gave her a hug. "We'll see you tonight, Vali. Try to get some rest."

She could have wept at the look of gratitude that washed over the singer's face and suddenly wished she could just bundle Vali up and take her home with her and Daniel. She guessed Vali Tremayne to be within a year or two of her own age, twenty-eight, and yet at times the sad young woman evoked a protective instinct in Jennifer nearly as strong as her maternal affection for little Jason.

David walked outside with Dan and Jennifer as they left the cottage. "I'm glad you're coming tonight," he said. "Vali's really very fond of both of you."

"She's so special," Jennifer said quickly. "I just wish last night had never happened. It must have been a nightmare for her."

"How . . . was she?" David asked hesitantly. "When you finally got to her, I mean?"

Jennifer hedged, not really wanting to reveal what she'd thought of Vali's emotional condition the night before.

Again, Daniel surprised her with his bluntness. "She was hysterical," he said quietly but decidedly. "It took at least ten minutes just to get her calmed down enough to find out what had happened."

Jennifer watched David carefully but couldn't gauge his response to Daniel's words. "But . . . you do believe her?"

"Believe her?" Daniel repeated.

"That what she said happened . . . *did* happen?"

"Absolutely," Daniel replied. "She was terrified." He paused, then said even more emphatically, "No, Vali, didn't imagine any of that. Someone scared her almost witless."

"And the phone lines *had* been cut, David," Jennifer reminded him.

The musician raked an unsteady hand through his already tousled hair. "I know it's best that she stay with Leda. But Vali will insist on coming back to the cottage as soon as possible. She's always afraid of imposing on someone, even Leda."

"David," Dan said abruptly, "do you have any idea who could be behind this? Has Vali had any particular problems with anyone lately? Someone who might be trying to get even?"

84

David gave a short, voiceless laugh. "Vali? No, there's nothing like that. For one thing, she's almost a recluse. She sees no one but me, Graham, and Leda, except when she goes to church. And for another, she'd walk a mile out of her way to avoid offending anyone. No," he repeated tersely, "Vali would never give anyone a reason to do this to her."

Dan said nothing for a moment. When he finally spoke, he sounded vaguely puzzled. "It seems to me that whoever was responsible for last night had no intention of hurting Vali. It was more a deliberate attempt by someone familiar with her emotional condition to stir her up—to terrorize her." Another thought seemed to strike him, and he added, "You know, I wouldn't be surprised if our runaway carousel wasn't the same kind of incident."

"Daniel, do you really think someone would go to that much trouble just to frighten Vali?" Jennifer asked in surprise.

When he didn't answer, Jennifer glanced at David, disturbed by the intense gaze he had fastened on Daniel. As if the composer suddenly realized she was watching him, he looked away, whispered an abrupt goodbye, then started down the beach toward his house.

9

Leda Alexander lived in a gothic house right off the pages of a Victorian novel. It loomed in shrouded, mysterious dignity on a corner lot in one of Sandusky's oldest and most graciously restored neighborhoods. Jennifer took one long look at its turrets and towers above the wraparound veranda and sighed longingly.

"Is that a sigh of appreciation or envy?" Dan asked as they started up the long narrow walkway to the front door.

"Both. It's *wonderful*, Daniel! It looks like a giant dollhouse."

Before Jennifer could press the bell, the massive oak door with its stained glass panels was thrown open. Vali stood just inside, smiling warmly at the two of them.

She goes with the house, Jennifer thought.

In a daintily flowered dress with puff shoulders and a petticoat skirt, Vali looked exquisitely feminine, romantically delicate, and extremely young. The two men in her life had already arrived and both were standing behind her, much like sentries at the castle gate, Jennifer mused dryly.

Graham, impressively well-groomed and proper as always, had exchanged his customary suit for a more casual navy pullover and cream slacks. His polite-but-distant smile was firmly in place as Jennifer and Dan entered.

David, in a pair of white jeans and his usual striped shirt, looked comfortable but still tired, Jennifer noticed. He grinned at her, then pulled a stick of gum from his shirt pocket.

Once inside the spacious, ornate entry hall, they were met by Leda. She dabbed at a flour smudge beside her nose, then dried her hands on a kitchen towel. "Where's your dog,

Daniel?" she asked in her blunt, strident voice.

"We left her at the cottage. I wasn't sure whether you'd appreciate having her in the house."

"Oh, she wouldn't be a problem at all!" Leda insisted. "I wish I'd thought to tell you to bring her. I love dogs."

"That's all right. We really can't stay too long."

"I don't think we want to hear that," she answered, firmly grasping his arm. "Let's go into the library. I put the snacks and punch in there." She flashed a quick smile at Jennifer before turning to guide Dan through the large double doors off the hall.

"What a wonderful room!" Jennifer exclaimed as they entered the library. A tasteful blend of fine hardwood, massive furniture, velvet drapes and intricate cornices, the room was sumptuous with rich, deep colors of rose and gold. It apparently served as a combination study and music room. Floor-to-ceiling bookcases were filled to capacity. A concert size ebony grand piano dominated a large space at the far end of the room, dwarfing a nearby synthesizer and music cabinet.

Leda stopped at a giant sideboard heaped with a variety of snacks and two towering punchbowls. "Here, Daniel—I've led you to the food. I'll run down the list and you can tell me what you'd like."

Appreciating the novelist's direct, comfortable attitude toward Daniel's blindness, Jennifer offered, "I can do that, Leda. I already know without asking what he'll want."

With an interested smile, Dan inclined his head toward his wife. "And what's that, Sherlock?"

"Well, for starters, Daniel, there's an enormous bowl of shrimp."

His eyes widened and so did his smile.

"Oh, Vali—I almost forgot." Jennifer reached in her purse and pulled out a small, gift-wrapped package. "For your birthday," she said.

With a shy smile, Vali took the gift and placed it on a long library table with some others. At Leda's instructions, she then went to get ice for the punch, taking Graham with her to fetch the coffee urn from the kitchen.

"Ah, Leda, Leda—you made the *baklava*." David stared down at a large tray of pastry, his eyes glinting with anticipation.

Jennifer turned to look. "What's that?"

"*Baklava*? It's a Greek pastry," Leda explained. "Have one."

Daniel beat her to it. Biting into one of the delicate sweets, his face lit up with pleased surprise. "Mm. I've never tasted anything like that. Did you make it yourself, Leda?"

"Yes. It takes forever. I used to make it more often; it was one of Paul's favorite . . . . " She stopped, glanced away for an instant, then brightened. "I'm glad you like it, Daniel. You and Jennifer can take some home with you tonight."

"I thought Jeff was coming," David said, reaching for a second pastry.

Leda glanced at the doorway Graham had just exited. "He'd planned to be here, but he called about an hour ago to say he isn't going to make it. A former client is in Port Clinton just until tomorrow, so they're having dinner tonight." She turned to Dan and Jennifer, explaining, "Jeff's my next-door neighbor. He's an attorney."

David gave Jennifer a conspiratorial wink. "Just moved in this summer, and already he's fallen for the girl next door."

Leda colored and darted a warning look at the mischievous composer. "David . . . . "

He grinned at her. "Hey—I'm cheering you on. A good man is hard to find, Leda. Go for it."

She shook her head in hopeless resignation, but Jennifer noticed that the smile she gave David was affectionate. "Well, it will save Graham glaring at the poor man all evening, anyway," she said wryly.

"Graham just hasn't accepted the fact," David said archly, "that his mother is still a young and attractive woman."

"That will get you all the *baklava* you want, young man," Leda said with a droll smile. She turned to Jennifer. "I think what Graham can't accept is my being interested in anyone other than his father. My husband died several years ago. Farrell was a wonderful man, but it *has* been years . . . . " She shook her head. "I can never predict Graham's reactions. Paul was easier," she said with a sigh. "Graham has always been so . . . complicated. But, then, they say he's a genius. I don't suppose," she added with a quick laugh, "there's any such thing as an uncomplicated genius."

A few minutes later, Jennifer tugged at Dan's arm and led him down to the other end of the room. "This piano is magnificent, Daniel." The lid was closed, but she couldn't resist touching the top of it gently. It was obviously an instrument crafted by experts.

Leda came to stand beside them. "This was Paul's piano," she said softly. "After the accident . . . I had it brought here." She paused. "Vali says you're both familiar with Paul's music."

Daniel nodded with a sad smile. "Familiar with it—and in awe of it. If your one son is a scientific genius, your other son was a musical genius, Mrs. Alexander."

"Please—call me Leda. Yes, I think you're right about Paul—he was definitely gifted," she said with quiet pride. "He was also a good son. A fine man."

Seeing the older woman's eyes mist, Jennifer reached out to touch her on the hand. "It was a terrible loss for you."

Leda gave a little shake of her head. "Yes. And for many others." She turned to look toward the other end of the room where Vali stood talking with Graham.

A few minutes later, Leda herded everyone into the dining room for cake and ice cream. Two enormous sheet cakes rested in the middle of a long walnut table. One was lavishly decorated and heaped high with fresh strawberries. The other was plain with white frosting and candy flowers.

Vali exclaimed with pleasure as she bent over the strawberry-topped cake. "Oh, Leda! It's beautiful!"

"This child is positively dippy about strawberries," Leda said, laughing at Vali's enthusiasm. "Graham," she said, turning to her son, "I got a cake for you, too. Graham is allergic to strawberries," she explained to Jennifer and Dan.

At Leda's request, David asked the blessing in his whisper-voice. When Jennifer opened her eyes after the prayer, she wasn't surprised to see Graham's face set in an expression of mild scorn.

Leda cut the strawberry cake, first handing a generous piece to Vali.

"No candles, Mother?" Graham asked.

"Oh, dear, I forgot!" Leda looked flustered.

Vali laughed and reached to squeeze the older woman's shoulder. "I don't need candles! Just give me the strawberries!"

Leda cut another piece, put it on a plate, and offered it to David, who hesitated, then shook his head. "I'm afraid I'll have to share Graham's cake. I don't tolerate strawberries very well, either."

Leda raised her eyes to his face. "Well, David—so you and Graham *do* have something in common after all, even if it is only an allergy." A brief look of dry amusement crossed her face.

David stared at her for a moment. A hint of mischief leaped in his eyes, and he said, "I think Graham and I have more in common than you might realize, Leda."

The novelist lifted her dark brows. "Mm. Yes, that's likely so," she agreed, glancing at her son, who stood behind Vali, looking as if his face had been chiseled from stone.

After they ate, Vali opened her presents. Conspicuous by its absence was a gift from Graham. Jennifer wondered about this until she saw him draw Vali to one side and say quietly, "My gift for you is private, dear. I'll give it to you tomorrow night at dinner, when we're alone." Vali paled at his words, appearing to be, Jennifer thought, more disturbed than pleased.

It was David's gift, wrapped in a thin package resembling a stationery box, that seemed to give Vali the most pleasure.

With a puzzled smile, Vali unwrapped it and lifted a few sheets of paper from within, staring at them for a long time before finally lifting her eyes to look at David. "You wrote this for me?"

He studied her expression anxiously, then smiled at her. "With a title like *Vali's Song*, it must be for you."

They continued to stare at each other. Jennifer couldn't resist a covert glance at Graham. His face was red, his mouth a tight line, his eyes glazed with what could only be anger.

Leda broke the silence. "What a nice thing to do, David! But this is a gift that's meant to be shared, Vali. Won't you sing it for us, darling?"

Vali cast a startled glance at the older woman. "Oh—I don't think so . . . "

David rose from the footstool where he'd been perched. Still smiling, he crossed the few feet between them, took her hand, and pulled her up from her chair. "Leda's right, princess. That magnificent voice of yours is meant to be shared." His eyes never left her face. "Sing your song for us, Vali. Please."

Everyone but Graham added their own appeal to David's. Vali hesitated, looking from David to the piano down at the other end of the room. Finally, she seemed to make her decision, squaring her shoulders and giving Leda a ghost of a smile. "I haven't sung for anyone other than David for so long—"

91

"What better time to begin than now, when you're surrounded by people who care for you—and with a song that was written just for you?" Leda asked softly.

Gently, David began to propel her toward the piano, the others following. With obvious reluctance, Vali allowed herself to be led.

"Will you play it for me first?" she asked him as he propped up the lid on the grand.

"Of course." He smiled at her and eased himself onto the piano bench.

When she would have handed him the music, he shook his head, smiling as he began softly strumming, then running through a random variety of chord progressions with no particular pattern. He stopped once, glancing up at Leda as if a thought had just struck him. "Are you sure it isn't going to bother you—my playing Paul's piano?"

Leda met his gaze. "No. Paul allowed all his friends to use the piano. Even their children." She gave him a small, sad smile. "He always said . . . that a musical instrument was worthless when it was silent."

Jennifer saw the composer study Leda's face with a look of tenderness and understanding. Even as he watched her, his hands began to caress the keys with the touch of a master, finally settling into a plaintive, haunting melody. "This is your song, Vali," he said, the music now flowing effortlessly from his confident hands.

At first, Vali silently scanned the music as David played. But it wasn't long before she began to gently sway with the rhythm and hum softly. Soon she was singing the words, faintly at first, then with more strength and assurance. Finally, the unforgettable voice that had made her famous began to wrap its incredible power and richness around the melody, almost as if she had no way of stopping it from doing what it was meant to do.

Jennifer held her breath as she clung to Daniel's hand,

listening to the voice she'd thrilled to for years on recordings. She heard his deep sigh of admiration and knew he shared her soaring feelings.

The song was achingly beautiful, an unforgettable tribute to the singer that stopped just short, Jennifer thought, of being a love song. When it was over, there was a long silence before everyone—everyone but Graham—exploded into applause and mingled outbursts of appreciation.

Jennifer glanced at David and caught her breath at the expression on his face. She knew she would never forget the depth of emotion she saw in that look—the pain, the sorrow, and most of all, the love. At that moment, Jennifer knew that, whatever else David Nathan Keye might be, he was first of all a man consumed by love.

Everyone begged for more, and Vali complied, although at first with some hesitancy. The more she sang, however, the more Jennifer began to see an unveiling, an unfolding. Like a rose that had been buried in the snow over a long winter, the young singer opened herself a petal at a time, revealing what seemed to be a limitless amount of talent and power. Jennifer stood in dazed awe, clinging even more tightly to Daniel's hand, knowing she was watching the rebirth of a talent only God could have created.

So absorbed was she in the musical wonder taking place before her eyes, she was startled when Vali, still singing, pushed between her and Daniel and tugged them closer to the piano. David, grinning his approval, kept playing, but told Dan, "Have a piano, Daniel. I'll furnish the orchestra." He then scooted easily from the bench, guided Dan onto it, and turned to switch on the synthesizer beside the grand.

No slouch at a keyboard, Dan moved smoothly into the middle of the song David had been playing without missing more than a beat.

Vali linked her arm through Jennifer's. "This act needs a little harmony, Jennifer—and your husband says you're a great singer. Help me out."

Her mouth agape, Jennifer stared at Vali in astonishment. "Me? Sing . . . with *you*?"

"Hey—I'm not so bad," Vali kidded her. "Come on, Jennifer."

Their banter was lost in a thundering, driving cadence from the synthesizer. Dan took his cue from David, jumping quickly onto the upbeat, rousing tempo of a popular contemporary number. Dumbfounded at the position she now found herself in, Jennifer nevertheless launched into the song, surprised at how easy it was for her to fall into harmony with Vali. *Wait until our folks hear about this!* she thought, almost overcome with incredulous excitement.

They sang for the next twenty minutes. Jennifer, though she'd originally been trained in classical and operatic music, was an avid devotee of Christian contemporary music and knew every song Vali ran by her. She didn't miss the glowering look of disapproval Graham leveled at them while they were singing, but she was having too much fun to care. They stopped singing only once, to enjoy a friendly duel between Dan and David at their respective keyboards.

Daniel was a highly trained musician with a wealth of natural ability, and Jennifer felt herself about to explode with the pride and pleasure of watching him hold his own with one of the foremost musicians in the industry. David playfully challenged him, throwing one variation after another at him, each of which Dan met smoothly with an improvisation of his own. Finally, they blended their instruments together and broke into a medley of well-known praise numbers, bringing Jennifer and Vali back into the music, ending at last with Dan and even Leda singing along.

When they were done, Leda grabbed Vali and embraced her, unashamedly weeping. "It's been so long, darling . . . so long."

Only Graham stood back, watching them with an expression that clearly expressed his displeasure.

David turned off the synthesizer and reached to shake Dan's hand vigorously. "Daniel—why in the world aren't you in this business? You're *good*, man! Really good."

Dan's smile was modest but pleased. "I never wanted it. I have everything any man could ever hope for—and more." He turned his head in Jennifer's direction. "Much more."

David glanced from one to the other. "Well, I can tell you this: There are a lot of people already on the charts who would like to have some of your talent. At least keep up with your writing. Give us another *Daybreak*."

"I didn't actually write *Daybreak* because I wanted to, David," Dan said, rising from the piano bench. "I wrote it because I *had* to. I never thought of writing music. The station has been my ministry for years."

"And your counseling, too, Daniel," Jennifer reminded him.

David studied Dan's face with admiring interest. "What kind of counseling?"

"I just finished up a degree in Christian counseling a few weeks ago. Mostly I work with the blind."

"What a full life you have, Daniel," Vali said softly. "I don't know how you manage everything."

"I don't." Dan grinned and motioned to Jennifer at his side. "She does the managing." His expression turned serious. "One thing's for sure, Vali," he said. "There can't be any doubt about *your* ministry. What an absolutely incredible gift God has given you."

At that point, Graham stepped in, wrapping his arm possessively around Vali's shoulders. "We're all aware of that, Daniel," he said stiffly. "However, the frenzied pace of her career hasn't always proven . . . beneficial for Vali. That's why it's so important that she take her time and not rush into anything."

Jennifer saw something flicker in Dan's eyes, but his voice revealed nothing. "I can understand that."

David, watching the exchange, flashed an impish smile at Graham. "Ah, Graham . . . ever the careful, analytical scientist. We emotional musician types must really jar your equilibrium."

"The world needs all kinds," Graham returned smoothly.

David lifted both eyebrows in mock surprise, obviously readying his comeback.

As if she sensed a brewing confrontation, Leda moved in quickly. "Graham, would you and David help me for a moment, please? I need to move that sideboard back into the dining room."

Jennifer was surprised when Vali spoke up as soon as Leda and the two men left the room.

"Daniel . . . " She paused, looked at Jennifer, then went on in a soft, hesitant tone. "I was wondering . . . you said you're a counselor . . . ."

Dan nodded, giving her a questioning smile.

"I was wondering . . . would you . . . could I . . . talk with you . . . sometime? About . . . some things?"

Dan looked surprised. "Vali, most of my experience has been with people who are handicapped in some way—particularly the blind."

Vali didn't answer right away. When she finally spoke, her voice was low and strained. "Daniel, I *am* handicapped."

Jennifer touched her lightly on the arm. "Vali, I'll leave so you can talk to Daniel."

"No," she said quickly. "Please don't." She looked up at Dan again. "Daniel, I need help. There's something wrong . . . with my mind, I think."

He frowned. "Why would you think that?"

"Because of . . . a lot of things. I'm afraid, Daniel. I'm afraid most of the time. And I don't know what I'm afraid of. I pray and ask Christ to help me overcome my fear, but I never seem to get any better."

It occurred to Jennifer, as she watched the frail young singer clench and then relax her hands, that the contrast between the dynamic, joyful performer of a few moments before and the uncertain, faltering girl staring up at Daniel with a look of pleading desperation was almost incomprehensible.

"Vali, it takes a long time before a counselor can be of any help to a person," Dan said kindly. "We'll be going home in a few days."

"I know that," Vali said quickly. "But I thought perhaps you could at least—" She stopped. "I'm sorry. I can't seem to remember that the two of you are supposed to be on your honeymoon. I insist on barging into your life, don't I? I'm really sorry—please forget I said anything."

"No, Vali—that's all right." Dan's expression was troubled. "Listen, I'd be glad to talk with you. I just don't want to mislead you, that's all."

Vali didn't answer but stared miserably down at the floor.

"Vali—" Dan pressed gently. "Will you be coming back to your cottage soon, do you think?"

"Tomorrow, I hope. If everything is repaired by then."

"When you get back, why don't you give us a call—or just come over. We'll talk, okay?"

"Are you sure, Daniel? I hate asking you, but—"

"It's perfectly all right," Dan assured her. "You're a friend. Right, Jennifer?"

Jennifer reached out to clasp Vali's hand. "Daniel means it, Vali. You're not imposing. We want to help in any way we can."

Jennifer jumped in surprise at the unexpected sound of Graham's sharp voice. "I couldn't help but hear part of your conversation." He glanced angrily from Vali to Dan. "I must tell you that I think it's a very foolish idea, Vali."

"Graham—please, don't . . . . "

"If you feel the need for professional help, I strongly suggest that we consult a medical doctor," he interrupted. "I don't want to be rude, Daniel, or denigrate your ability," he continued coldly, "but as I heard you point out to Vali—you *will* be leaving soon. What disturbs me most," he said, returning his attention to Vali, "is that you haven't even discussed this with me."

David, returning to the room during Graham's protest, walked up behind the scientist and said, "Is there any particular reason why she should?"

Graham whirled around. "This is none of your business, Keye!"

David, seemingly unruffled, clucked his tongue and grinned wickedly. "Watch it, Graham. You're going to show some emotion here, if you're not careful."

"You insolent—"

"*Stop* it!" It was Leda—sharp, angry, and firm. "That's enough from both of you. This is Vali's birthday. David, you're a guest in my home, and a welcome one so long as you don't upset Vali. Graham—you may be my son, but the same condition applies to you."

The determined thrust of her chin and her steady, censuring glare silenced both men.

"I'm sorry, Leda," David offered apologetically. "You're absolutely right—I was out of line."

Graham's eyes never left the musician's face as he muttered a grudging, "Sorry, Mother." He then turned to Vali. "But I meant what I said. Your emotions are too important to toy with, Vali. If you're serious about this, there are a couple of excellent men in the area who would accept you as a patient, I'm sure."

"For heaven's sake, Graham, I don't want to commit myself to an asylum! I just want to talk with someone— another Christian, preferably—who might be able to help me sort out my problems."

Jennifer, although astonished by Vali's outburst, silently applauded her.

Graham flinched, but his tight mask of control never slipped. After a long, awkward silence, he said, "We can talk about this tomorrow. I have to leave now; I still have notes to dictate tonight. Will you see me out?"

"I—yes, of course," Vali stammered, moving quickly toward the door without looking at anyone.

As soon as Vali returned to the room, Jennifer and Dan said their goodbyes and went to the car.

Jennifer was securing her seatbelt when she saw David and Vali walk out onto the porch together. He reached for her hand, said something, then released her and started down the walk toward his black Lincoln parked at the curb. With a brief wave in Jennifer's direction, he unlocked the car and got in.

Just before she started the car and pulled away, Jennifer looked once more at Vali standing alone on the porch. Again she felt an involuntary tug of concern. She frowned and shook her head as if to banish her increasingly strong feelings of apprehension for Vali Tremayne.

She turned the corner and headed for the highway. Glancing in the rearview mirror, she saw the headlights of David's car following close behind. Again Jennifer wondered about the enigmatic composer's role in Vali's life. Was he a part of the troubled young woman's problems, or—and she considered the possibility highly unlikely—could he possibly be a key to the solution?

10

At eleven o'clock that night, a man uttered a series of curt monosyllables into his telephone receiver. He shifted impatiently in his chair from time to time, waiting for a chance to make a statement.

Finally his opportunity came. "I think we need to do something about Kaine and his wife."

There was a long pause. Then, "I thought you said they were harmless."

"That was my first impression. But apparently he's some kind of . . . counselor." The man pulled in a deep breath of irritation and tugged at the collar of his shirt. "Vali mentioned something to him tonight about . . . having a talk with him."

The line was silent for an instant. "Why?"

The man glanced nervously around the room, focusing on a small photograph of Vali Tremayne. "She's becoming aware of her own instability. She said she feels the need for help."

"How did the blind man respond?"

"He agreed." Almost angrily, he rubbed the material of his collar back and forth between his thumb and index finger. "I think she's planning on trying to see him sometime tomorrow."

"I knew we should have acted on my original instincts," the voice at the other end of the line snapped.

"Just keep an eye on these snoops—I'll take care of the rest of it."

The other man said nothing for a moment. When he finally spoke again, his voice was oiled with a smirk. "You want her, don't you? You've fallen for her."

"I've never pretended to be completely indifferent to her."

100

"That's quite true, you haven't. Up to now, however, you've shown an admirable restraint of your feelings."

"My feelings are my business."

"Only if they don't interfere with the work."

"They never have, have they?"

"Not until recently." He paused. "All right; continue as you wish for now. We'll take care of Kaine and his woman."

"Be careful. The man is no fool."

"Don't worry, we'll be discreet. Just get on with your part." After a petulant sigh, he added, "All these complications annoy me. You used to be such an easy man to work with. Lately, you've become troublesome. *Do* try to be somewhat less tiring, won't you?"

The man hung up, slouched deeper in his chair, and scowled at the photograph beside him. It was true that he wasn't entirely mindless of her appeal. Still, he had no intention whatever of allowing her to complicate his life any more than she already had. Like anyone else who got in the way of the work, she was expendable.

11

The ferry from Catawba to Middle Bass Island wasn't crowded. It was a week day, and the tourist season was at an end. Still, there were several people aboard, enough to provide a steady hum of conversation; that and the engine noise made it necessary for Jennifer to speak in a louder than normal tone.

"I think we're going to have another beautiful day," she told Dan, hooding her eyes with one hand as she glanced up into the bright, cloudless sky.

They were sitting on metal benches on the outer deck. Jennifer had tied a bandana over her hair to protect it from the spray off the lake. Dan held a large picnic basket in his lap.

"What's for lunch?" he asked, tapping the cover of the basket.

"All kinds of good stuff from that deli up the road. I bought fried chicken, potato salad, ham and cheese, rolls—oh, and a pound cake."

"Hm. We'll have to take a doggie bag back to Sunny."

"Poor thing; she hasn't had much fun on this trip," Jennifer said, linking her arm through Dan's. "But what would we do with her when we rent a bike?"

Dan pulled his mouth into a skeptical line. "We're really going to do this, huh? The tandem bike, I mean."

"That's the best way to see the island, Daniel."

"I can't *see* the island, Jennifer," he reminded her dryly. "And you've already seen it. So why can't we just walk around for a while and then eat?"

"Biking is good exercise, Daniel. You were grumbling just yesterday about needing exercise." She patted her flat abdomen. "And so do I. You're not worried about riding a bike, are you?"

He grinned. "You're probably the one who should be worried, darlin'. Having me along may cramp your style just a little."

"Not a chance. It'll be fun. And romantic. There's something very romantic about a bicycle built for two."

"Jennifer, take my word for it. There is nothing even remotely romantic about a grown man taking a tumble into the bushes. Even if the woman he loves is right behind him."

"Daniel, any man who isn't afraid to ride the *Gemini* can't possibly be intimidated by a bicycle."

"Wanna bet?"

She elbowed him and turned to survey their fellow passengers. Directly across from them sat two young Oriental men with cameras strapped around their necks. On the same row of seats were an elderly man and woman. The woman had little round wire-rimmed glasses perched on an upturned nose and was smiling at Jennifer wisely, as if she could tell she was a newlywed.

Jennifer returned the woman's smile, then let her gaze move further up the deck. A middle-aged man with a briefcase was reading a science fiction paperback. A few seats away three college-aged girls were deep in conversation.

Had her attention not been caught by the flaming red hair of one of the girls, Jennifer probably would never have noticed the man standing close to them. Her admiring glance went from the curly hair of the coed to the glistening bald dome of the burly man towering above her. He looked familiar somehow, and when he moved, she caught a better glimpse of his profile.

She gasped, staring at him with astonishment. *He looked like the man she'd seen at Cedar Point!* Suddenly he moved toward the corner of the deck and disappeared. Jennifer craned her neck, then quickly stood up. She took a few steps away from the bench, her eyes scanning the passengers carefully. But he was nowhere in sight.

"Jennifer?" Dan's puzzled voice reminded her that he couldn't know what she was doing.

She came back and sat down, now turning her gaze to the people inside the passenger cabin. Silently she searched the faces of the crowd. She finally gave up, telling herself she was being foolish.

"Honey? Is something wrong?"

"No, nothing," she answered quickly, reaching over to squeeze his hand. "I was just looking around. I thought I saw someone I recognized."

Of course, it wasn't the same man. And even if it was, what would that prove? For goodness' sake, dummy, don't go getting paranoid about a bald-headed man!

Still, she continued to study the passengers on the ferry, half-hoping she wouldn't see the man again, yet at the same time disturbed by his abrupt disappearance.

"Well—did you or didn't you enjoy the bicycle ride?" Jennifer asked smugly as she pitched their napkins and paper plates into a nearby trash receptacle.

Dan stood up from the picnic table bench. He stretched his arms over his head, yawned, and pushed up the sleeves of his cotton shirt. "It was an experience, I have to admit."

"Is this the first time you've been on a bike since the accident?"

He nodded. "Gabe has tried to talk me into it a couple of times, but I didn't take to the idea."

"But you do so many other things," she pointed out. "You told me you go horseback riding with the kids at the Farm. And you bowl. And swim, of course."

"Speaking of swimming—"

"You've already spoken of swimming," Jennifer interrupted. "Several times, as a matter of fact. I'm beginning to think my competition is going to be a pool."

"You'll never have any competition, kid. But you know what they say—if you can't beat 'em . . . "

"So you can laugh me out of the pool again, like you did at Gatlinburg last week? No thanks."

"I didn't laugh at you," he protested indignantly. "Is it my fault you got your feelings hurt the third time I had to haul you in from the shallows?"

"I told you before we ever got married that I'm not a fish," she said self-righteously.

"But you *didn't* tell me," he countered with a smirk, "that you still used an inner tube." At her silence, he added, "Don't worry about it, darlin'. As soon as we get back to Shepherd Valley, you're going to have yourself some private lessons. You'll be Olympic material in no time."

She rolled her eyes skeptically. "I'll settle for learning how to negotiate a decent front crawl."

Walking around to her side of the table, Dan reached for her hand. He pulled her to his side, draping an arm around her shoulder. "Find us a tree, love."

"A tree?" She stared at him blankly, then caught on. "You're about to take a nap, right?"

"Ten minutes?"

"I'm wise to your ten minute snoozes, Daniel," she said, leading him over to an enormous old cottonwood tree and dropping down to lean against its trunk with him. "It's like trying to wake a grizzly in December."

Wrapped securely in Dan's arms, Jennifer rested against the broad shelter of his chest and glanced around their surroundings with lazy contentment. The picnic area was a quiet, secluded little glen. A warm spray of sunshine trickled through the trees overhead. The air was tangy with the faint,

105

damp smell of the lake. It was a special time and a special place, and, at least for now, it belonged to them.

"Are you happy, Jennifer?" Dan asked quietly, tightening his embrace.

"Oh, Daniel—if I were any happier, I'd . . . I'd explode!"

He rested his chin on top of her head. "Have I thanked you today for marrying me?"

"Mm. I think so. Once or twice, anyway." She tipped her head to look up at him. His smile was soft and thoughtful. "What about you, Daniel? Are you happy?"

Enfolding her even more snugly in his arms, he pressed his lips to a slightly damp, heavy wave of hair at her temple. "Ah, love . . . *happy* just isn't a big enough word for the way I feel." He paused. "You know, before the Lord brought you into my life, I used to wake up every morning, after the accident, and for the first few minutes I had to literally *force* myself to face reality again, to . . . *condition* my mind all over again to the darkness. Even after five years of it, it was still hard for me to put on the truth each morning and start all over."

He brushed a gentle kiss into her hair. "But now . . . now I wake up, and I lie there, listening to you breathing so soft and easy right beside me . . . I feel your warmth, and I think about our love . . . and I don't mind the darkness anymore. Now I wake up to sunshine every morning."

Jennifer's eyes misted with happy tears, and she lifted her face for his kiss. Afterward, she sighed, and pressed her face against his shoulder. "Oh, Daniel . . . let's always love each other like this. Let's never, ever let our love get old or stale or—predictable."

He smiled at the depth of emotion in her voice, and there was a light chuckle in his tone when he answered. "Darlin'," he murmured into her hair, "somehow, I find it hard to believe that anything about our love . . . or life with you . . . will ever be predictable."

106

He kissed her again, and she snuggled as closely as possible to him. After several minutes of silence, she turned in his arms to look up at him. "Daniel, what do you think about Vali? Do you think she's right about there being something wrong with her mind?"

He shook his head. "No, I don't think so. Oh, there's something wrong," he added quickly. "But if you're asking me if I think Vali has mental problems, I don't."

"Then why do you think she said what she did last night at Leda's?"

"What I think," he replied thoughtfully, "is based on some things David told me as well as my own impressions. Vali seems to be extremely insecure about herself. David says that she has very little, if any, sense of her own worth. That's probably why she comes across as being so shy and uncertain." His tone was gloomy when he added, "As serious as that is, it may not be the whole problem."

"What do you mean?" Seeing his grim expression, Jennifer felt her own concern deepen.

When he didn't answer right away, Jennifer prompted him. "Daniel? What are you thinking?"

"I wish I could see her eyes," he replied slowly with a small frown. "There's something not right about the way she talks, but I'm not sure what it is. Haven't you noticed," he asked her, "how sometimes her voice has almost no inflection? Not always," he said quickly, "but once in a while she sounds like she's talking in a vacuum. There's a . . . a flatness in her voice. And the way she stumbles over her words. Doesn't that strike you as peculiar for a singer?"

Jennifer stared hard at him. He was right. She would never have realized it if Dan hadn't mentioned it first, but he had just pinpointed one of the things she'd found vaguely disconcerting about Vali from the beginning.

"Yes. I think I know what you mean," she agreed slowly.

107

"But it isn't all that noticeable. Why? Do you think it means something?"

He nodded. "I think it's probably one of two things—and if I could see her eyes, I might know which. That lack of expression and nuance in her voice could indicate a significant emotional problem, like depression. Or, it could be that she's on some kind of tranquilizer."

Surprised, Jennifer asked, "You don't think Vali is taking drugs, do you?"

He shook his head. "Not the way you're thinking. She could be taking a prescription drug under a physician's care."

"But you don't think so." Jennifer saw the doubt in his expression. "Do you?"

He hesitated before answering. "I don't think it's likely that Vali would have asked me for help if she were already seeing a doctor for her problems. Besides, Graham made it perfectly clear that she isn't."

"Well, whatever it is," Jennifer said with assurance as she settled back into his embrace, "I know you'll be able to help her."

He rubbed his chin across the top of her head. "Don't be so sure, Jennifer. It's not likely I'll have time to even find out what the problem is, much less help solve it. I only agreed to talk with her because I thought I might be able to direct her to the kind of doctor who *can* help."

They were silent for a long time, each thinking their own thoughts. Jennifer couldn't help but wonder if either of the two men in Vali's life played a part in her problems. Then she puzzled over which man might be the negative influence. Or could *both* of them be having a destructive effect on the troubled singer?

Finally, she felt Dan's breathing grow even and shallow and turned to glance up at him. She smiled when she saw that he was sleeping and moved to kiss him gently on his bearded cheek. Then she gave a long sigh and burrowed more comfortably into his arms for a short nap of her own.

Half an hour later, the man watching them through field glasses saw them get up, tie their windbreakers around their waists, and put the rest of their picnic supplies in the basket on the bike. After a quick look around the area, they got on the tandem bike, the blind man on the seat in back of the woman.

The man lowered the field glasses and sprinted to the large dark sedan parked a few feet away. He brought the powerful engine to life, not waiting for the idle to slow before pulling out onto the narrow road.

As soon as he had them in view, he slowed the car, staying at least a quarter of a mile behind them.

He followed them at that distance for no more than five minutes, continuously checking the rearview mirror. There was no one else on the road. Glancing from one side of the road to the other and seeing no pedestrians, he applied a little more pressure to the accelerator, keeping the couple on the bike in sight. Staring straight ahead, he lowered the gas pedal even more. Suddenly he floored it, and the big, powerful car belched a loud roar, then hurled forward, directly toward the tandem bike ahead.

Jennifer heard the sound of the engine and glanced back over her shoulder to see what was happening. She panicked at the sight of the car homing in on them and uttered a choked cry of alarm. The bike swerved sharply to the left.

"Jennifer? What is it?" Dan put a steadying hand on her shoulder.

She swung her head around. Facing forward, she tried to pedal faster, then turned to look behind them once more. "There's a car—coming straight at us!"

A wave of terror swept through her. The sedan was

barreling down on them like an angry black tornado.

For a split second, Jennifer froze and almost lost control of the bike. Her hands gripping the handlebars began to shake, and her throat constricted with panic.

"Dan—*he's going to hit us!*"

Staring back in shocked disbelief, Jennifer didn't see the deep chuckhole in the road until the bike hit it full force. Stunned, she heard Dan cry out, felt him grab for her, heard the squeal of tires and her own shriek of terror as the bike flew off the road and crashed into a deep, stone-filled ditch.

Jennifer caught a flying glimpse of the driver behind the wheel of the speeding sedan as he roared past them without slowing. He snapped his head around to look at them, lying helplessly in the ditch, and in that fleeting instant she saw that he had pale eyes and no hair.

12

When the phone rang late the next morning, Dan answered it. Jennifer was in the bathroom applying ointment to the scratches on her face and arms. She hadn't exaggerated when she told Dan she looked as if she'd been dragged across a gravel road.

Dan had somehow emerged from the bicycle crash without a scratch, although he'd wrenched a shoulder and bruised a rib or two. He'd done his best to absorb most of the fall, holding on to Jennifer and trying to keep her on top as they were thrown into the ditch. But the impact threw her away from him at the last minute.

Once the shock had worn off, they got up and started walking, leaving the bicycle behind. After reporting the incident to the attendant at the bike rental, they called the police from a pay phone. The officer who came out to the pier to talk with them was polite and concerned, but offered little hope for finding the man who had tried to run them down. Without a license number or specific description of the car, it would be difficult to trace the driver.

Much later, after they'd returned to the cottage, Jennifer told Dan about the driver of the car, that she was positive he had been the same man who had aroused her suspicions at Cedar Point. She told him, too, that she was now certain he had been on the ferry with them that morning.

Dan had been quiet for a long time. Finally he told her, with obvious reluctance, that he felt there was a definite link between the problems they'd had at the amusement park, the intruder at Vali's cottage, and the incident with the car.

He'd gone on to hint of something even more frightening, his tone grim and a little angry as he told her what he suspected. "I think someone is either trying to scare Vali out of her wits—or worse, trying to . . . hurt her. I think she's in real danger." He paused. His next words made Jennifer shiver and grasp his hand tightly. "I also think we've been caught up in it, whatever's going on. I don't know why—but we're in the net, I'm sure of it."

Jennifer was staring accusingly at herself in the mirror when Dan walked into the bathroom. "Honey, are you sure you don't need to see a doctor?"

"Oh, no—I'm all right." She put the tube of ointment back on the top shelf of the medicine cabinet and turned to him. "Who was on the phone?"

"Vali. She wanted to know if she could come over—or if we'd mind coming over to her place. I told her what had happened and that you're kind of sore, so she's going to walk over here in a few minutes. Okay?"

"Sure, that's fine. Only—"

"What?"

She sighed. "I'm beginning to feel really guilty about all this."

Dan closed the distance between them and reached for her hand. "What are you talking about?"

"It's my fault that we're caught up in this mess. If I hadn't been so curious our first day up here, we probably wouldn't have people trying to run us down."

"That's a little irrational, even for you, sweetheart."

"Thanks," she answered wryly.

"I mean it." He rested both hands on her shoulders. "In the first place, we can't be sure what happened yesterday has anything to do with Vali."

"You as much as said you thought it did, Daniel."

"And in the second place," he continued evenly, "even if it is related, you didn't go looking for it."

"Mm. Well, whether I went looking for it or not, I've sure managed to foul up our honeymoon."

For a moment he stood unmoving, as if he were seriously considering her words. Then a trace of a smile touched his lips as he framed her face between his hands. "I don't know about you, darlin'," he said softly, "but *I* think our honeymoon has been nothing short of wonderful."

She looked up at him. "You do?"

"Absolutely," he whispered. With infinite tenderness, he scanned her face with his fingertips, a mannerism she'd grown to love. Gently, he brushed a heavy wave of hair away from her cheek. Still smiling the sweet, soft little smile that never failed to make her heart spin, he pressed a kiss on her forehead. She closed her eyes, and he kissed them, too. Then she smiled, and he kissed her lips. For a long time.

At last he lifted his face from hers with a little sound of regret.

"Then you're not feeling neglected?" she murmured.

He touched one finger to her mouth and shook his head. "A little crowded maybe. Husbands are like that, you know."

"I'm afraid I don't know very much about husbands yet," Jennifer confessed softly into the warmth of his shoulder.

"Ah, you're doing fine, darlin'," he murmured, pressing his lips gently against her cheek. "You're doing just fine."

Dan could hear the strain and uncertainty in Vali's voice as soon as she arrived at the cottage. She quickly dismissed Jennifer's offer to leave—almost too quickly, Dan thought, wondering if she already regretted her plea for help.

In spite of Vali's protests, though, Jennifer left her and Dan to talk alone in the kitchen, explaining her need to soak away some of her soreness in a hot tub.

After Jennifer left, Vali avoided the reason she'd come, attempting to make small talk with Dan.

Not surprised by her ambivalence, he finally took the lead.

"I thought we might hear from you yesterday," he said. "When did you come back to the cottage?"

"Early this morning. The phone was in service again by yesterday morning, but it took longer to get the door fixed."

"I don't imagine it was easy, coming back after that incident with the prowler."

She hesitated. "It was awful. I felt . . . . "

"Violated?" he prompted quietly.

"Yes—that's it exactly! It's as if somebody had intruded not only on my privacy, but on my *self*—my person—as well."

Dan nodded with understanding. "I'm sure you could have stayed with Leda a while. She seems to be extremely fond of you."

"Oh, Leda is wonderful," Vali said quickly. "And I love her as much as if she were my own mother—" she stopped, then went on, "at least, I think I do. I never knew my mother."

Over the next few minutes, she explained to Dan that her natural parents had abandoned her when she was still a toddler, and that she had grown up in foster homes until she was adopted at fourteen by a Nashville policeman and his wife.

Dan knew she was evading what she really wanted to talk about, but he also understood her reticence.

"Do you still see your adoptive parents?"

"Uncle Bill—that's what I called him—died just before I graduated from college. Aunt Mary still lives in Nashville, but I call her at least once a week."

Finally, Dan leaned back in his chair, crossed his arms over his chest, and gave her an encouraging smile. "Vali, what did you mean the other night at Leda's? When you told

114

me you were afraid, but you don't understand what you're afraid of?"

He heard her deep intake of breath, as if she hadn't expected his directness.

She attempted a shaky laugh. "After everything that's happened lately, I'm beginning to think I have more reason to be frightened than I guessed."

"But that isn't what you meant the other night, is it?" Dan asked gently.

She hesitated. "No," she admitted after a long pause. "It's just that sometimes . . . often . . . I feel frightened. Anxious. Almost . . . terrified." She faltered, then went on. "It's as if I'm expecting something to happen, something awful, something that I can't control. But I don't know what it is."

Dan frowned. "You say this happens often—how often, Vali?"

"Oh . . . I don't know . . . maybe once every couple of days. Yes," she said after a moment, "at least that."

"And you have no idea why?"

"No," she replied dejectedly. "I try as hard as I can to remember, but . . . . ."

He interrupted her. "Why do you say 'remember?' "

She didn't answer right away. When she finally spoke, Dan heard a note of surprise in her voice. "I just realized that . . . whatever it is I dread so terribly . . . I think it's something that happened a long time ago . . . something bad."

Dan leaned forward on his chair. He was quiet for a long time, lightly rapping his fingers on the tabletop as he thought about what she'd said.

"Do you remember when you first started to have these . . . anxiety attacks, Vali?"

After a long pause, Vali answered in a near-whisper. "Yes, I remember. It was . . . . " She stopped, then abruptly asked, "You know about Paul's death—the plane crash?"

Dan nodded.

"After Paul died, I had—they said I had a breakdown. I was in a sanitarium for months . . . I don't remember exactly how long."

Dan suddenly became aware of the gradual change in her voice. She was dropping back into the flat, expressionless tone he'd heard before. The longer she talked, he noticed, the more pronounced the monotone became.

"After I was well enough to leave the sanitarium, I stayed with Leda for a few weeks. Then I bought my cottage here at the lake."

It was as if she'd forgotten his question. "But when did you start feeling . . . afraid?" Dan prompted gently.

"Afraid?" She was silent for a long time. When she finally answered, her voice had cleared and sounded stronger. "It was while I was still at Leda's, I think. Yes," she said with more assurance, "it started then. I remember, because I had to start taking the medicine again."

"Medicine? What medicine was that?"

"Let's see, what did Graham call it? I don't remember. It was some kind of tranquilizer he got from Dr. Devries at the sanitarium."

"Your doctor prescribed it?"

"I suppose so. He gave Graham some samples the day I left the sanitarium. Once Graham found out what the medication was, he got a generic brand of the same thing from one of the doctors at the Center."

"The Center?"

"Graham's laboratory."

"They have medical doctors there, too?"

"Oh, yes. Graham says that more than half of the research men are medical doctors. They even have psychiatrists and psychologists."

"I see." Something flashed briefly in Dan's mind, then fled.

116

"What exactly does Graham do, Vali? What kind of research is he in?"

"Oh, Daniel," she said, laughing a little at herself, "I'm afraid I don't understand it well enough to tell you. It's all very technical. Graham is primarily a chemist, I believe. He more or less oversees the research at the Center. They do a number of different things, mostly with pharmaceutical research and development, I think."

Dan nodded slowly. "This medicine, Vali—Graham takes care of getting it for you?"

"That's right. I've tried to pay for it any number of times, but he won't let me. He says they get tons of samples at the Center and I might just as well use some of it. I really don't like taking things from him—he and Leda have already done so much for me—but he refuses to let me pay."

"That's understandable. Graham is very . . . fond of you, isn't he, Vali?"

"Yes," she admitted softly. "He wants to marry me. In fact . . . ."

When her voice drifted off, Dan prompted her again. "What, Vali?"

"He . . . bought a ring. Last night he took me to dinner. And he had the ring with him."

Dan lifted his brows in a question. "Are you wearing it now?"

"No. Not yet." Her reply was so soft he could barely hear it.

"Do you want to marry Graham, Vali? Or would you rather I not ask you that?"

"It's all right," she said, her voice still hardly more than a whisper. "I'm . . . very confused about my feelings for Graham sometimes."

Dan waited, saying nothing.

"I still . . . can't seem to forget about Paul."

After a moment, Dan replied, "I don't think anyone would expect you to forget him." He paused, then went on. "You loved Paul Alexander a great deal, didn't you, Vali?" he asked softly.

"He was my life," she said in a surprisingly strong, fervent tone.

Dan nodded, feeling a wave of compassion for her. "But I'm sure he'd want you to be happy, to love again, after all this time."

"I *want* to!" Her harsh outburst startled Dan. "I *want* to love Graham. He looks after me. He's wonderfully good to me . . . I *owe* it to him to love him."

Dan measured his words very carefully. "Vali, you can't use love to pay a debt."

He heard her voice falter. "I know . . . it's just that I want *so much* to love Graham. Sometimes I wish David had never come up here. I—" She stopped as if she hadn't meant to say what she did.

"David?" Dan frowned and rubbed his hand over his chin. "How is David complicating things for you?"

For a moment he wondered if he'd overstepped. But she answered him in a halting, uncertain tone. "He . . . cares for me, too." She paused, then added, "At least, he says he does."

"And that disturbs you?"

"David is a . . . disturbing man." She paused. "Some-times . . . sometimes he reminds me of Paul."

"Do you think that's why you're attracted to him?"

"I'm not!" She stopped, then said softly, "That's not true. I *am*. But I don't think it's because he's like Paul. The very things I felt drawn to in Paul seem to . . . to intimidate me in David." She laughed weakly. "That doesn't make sense, does it?"

Dan shrugged. "Our feelings often don't make sense, I'm afraid."

118

"I just don't understand my reaction to David. Sometimes I like to be with him . . . he makes me feel good about myself, like Paul always did. He makes me feel . . . special." There was a slight tremor in her voice as she went on. "But sometimes he almost . . . frightens me. I get this feeling when I'm with him . . . that there's something I need to know about him, something important, but . . . . " She broke off, then choked out a rush of words in frustration. "Oh, I don't know *what* I mean!"

Dan could hear the growing strain in her voice. The confused clutter of emotions he had sensed in Vali over the last hour troubled him. The young woman sitting across from him was so complex, her emotional state so frag-mented, that he felt a distinct need to get away from her in order to sort out what he had heard and try to make some sense of it.

As honestly—and as gently—as possible, he explained to her his need for time to think. "And there's something I want you to be thinking about, too, Vali," he told her. "What you said, about Paul—and David—making you feel good about yourself, making you feel special . . . that's good, having people who care about you and make you feel important to them. But it's absolutely vital that you realize that you *are* special, no matter what anyone else may think."

"I'm sorry," she said, "I don't understand."

"I know you don't. That's why I want you to think about this: You can't—and you don't have to—base your identity on what another person thinks about you." He leaned forward, intent on making her understand. "You *are* special, Vali—very special—because you're a child of God. Because He made you. Because He saved you. Because He loves you. It's your relationship to *Him* that makes you what you are, who you are—and enables you to be everything you can be."

He folded his hands on top of the table, lifted his chin

slightly, then said, "Let me give you just a couple of things to think about and pray about, okay? If you have any question about what you are in the eyes of the Lord, read Psalm 139 . . . *'For thou didst form my inward parts, Thou didst weave me in my mother's womb. I will give thanks to Thee, for I am fearfully and wonderfully made; wonderful are Thy works, and my soul knows it very well.'* "

He smiled at her. "One of my personal favorites is I John 3:1. *'See how great a love the Father has bestowed upon us, that we should be called children of God; and such we are.'* "

He thought for a minute, then added, "Remember this, Vali, you count . . . you matter. If you weren't important to another soul on this earth, you'd still be someone very special. Not so much because you're *you*—but more because you're *His*."

Vali was silent for a long time, and Dan let her think. Finally, she said, very simply, "Daniel . . . I'm not sure, but I think you may have just given me a very precious gift." He sensed the unshed tears in her voice.

There was something else he felt a need to bring up before she left. "Vali, one more thing. I'm a little concerned about this medication you're taking. You don't really know what it is, and . . . . "

Instantly defensive, she stopped him. "Graham wouldn't give me anything harmful, Daniel."

He made a quick dismissing gesture with one hand. "I'm not suggesting anything like that. I'm sure Graham means to help you. But you've been taking it for a long time without knowing anything about it. I'd be interested in seeing how you feel after a few days without it. Would you be willing to try?"

Her reply was slow in coming. "I suppose . . . if you don't think it would hurt me. But I only take one pill every other day, Daniel."

He thought that a peculiar dosage but said nothing. "When do you take it? What time of day?"

"Just before I go to bed."

"Did you have one last night?"

"No."

"So you'd be due to take a pill tonight?"

"That's right."

"How about skipping tonight's dosage? To see how you feel tomorrow?"

"Well . . . I suppose it would be all right."

Dan stood up. "If you start feeling bad or get uneasy about it, let me know. If you have any side effects at all, we'll get in touch with a doctor right away. But try to go through tonight and tomorrow without it, okay?"

She pushed her chair back and got up. "All right. But I doubt that I'll notice any difference, Daniel. Graham said it's very mild." She walked around the table. "I really should be getting back to the cottage now. David will be coming by soon to rehearse."

"How's it going? Have you made any decision yet about your career?"

He could hear the frustration in her voice when she answered. "David's music makes it awfully tempting. To tell you the truth, this is the first time since . . . since Paul died that I've begun to feel a desire—a need—to sing again. But . . . ."

When she didn't finish her thought, Dan completed it for her. "You don't know if you can handle it—emotionally?"

She sighed. "That's right." After a slight hesitation, she added, "And Graham doesn't want me to go back. He wants us to be married soon and live up here."

He walked to the door with her. Sunny got up from her rug by the sink and followed them. "Well, speaking from the standpoint of a radio man, I'm going to be hoping for a new album from you real soon. And speaking as a friend, I feel

121

exactly the same way. I can't help but hope that a gift like yours will be shared."

"Thanks, Daniel," she said, going out the door. "And thank you . . . so much . . . for listening to me. Tell Jennifer I'll talk with her later."

After she'd gone, Dan returned to the table and sat down. He was vaguely aware of Jennifer singing in the bathroom, then he heard her turn on the blow dryer.

He raked a hand through his hair and sighed. Out of the entire conversation with Vali, two things in particular troubled him. One was her comment about sometimes feeling afraid of David, and the other was his discovery that she'd been taking a medication for years without a doctor's continual supervision. What bothered him most about the latter fact was Graham Alexander's involvement. If he cared as much for Vali as he tried to make her believe, shouldn't he be a little more conscientious about giving her pills from his lab's supply of samples?

He admitted to himself that he was just as put off by the scientist as Jennifer seemed to be. It bothered Dan, however, that he and Jennifer were apparently at odds in their feelings about David Nathan Keye. Jennifer had been candid from the beginning about her conflicting feelings toward David, while Dan still instinctively trusted the man. He had to admit, however, that his instincts could be wrong. He couldn't gauge Keye's facial expressions or body language as Jennifer could. He tended to be cautious about trusting David too much, but he had to admit he'd been silently cheering the composer on in the contest for Vali's affection.

This was one of the times he felt more keenly than usual the restrictive nature of his handicap. While he knew the Lord had given him a certain amount of discernment, he also realized he would probably never feel totally secure in his sightless perceptions of people.

Except, of course, for his perception of his wife, who suddenly interrupted his reverie by sliding onto his lap, the sweet, sunshine fragrance of her hair falling across his face as she planted a kiss on his cheek. His vision of Jennifer was different. God had wondrously placed a picture of her in his heart right from the beginning—a picture painted with divine perfection and the unerring accuracy of love.

13

The troubled, fragmented dreams began that same night. Vali awoke in a panic after the first one, bolting upright in bed, gasping for breath, her heart pounding wildly.

She had seen Paul. But not the way she remembered him. His face had been angry, thunderous; his mouth set in a thin, hard line; his light gray eyes scalding with rage. His usually laughing face had loomed before her like a glowering, threatening mask.

She looked groggily at the digital clock beside the bed and saw that it was only three a.m. For another half-hour she tossed restlessly, unsettled by the dream. When she finally fell asleep again, it was with a heavy heart and a troubled mind.

But the dreams began again, like a loosely connected stream of moving pictures forcing themselves upon her. Terrible pictures of the plane crash assaulted her, pictures she'd seen in the newspapers after Paul had been killed, and pictures she had only imagined during the long, hazy nights at the sanitarium. Flashes of fire, the plane ablaze, everything burned, destroyed, disintegrated. The burning plane, Paul inside the plane. *No remains*, an oily, menacing voice whispered inside her head. *Everything burned . . . nothing but ashes . . . no remains . . . .*

This time she was sick when she awakened, her stomach pitching, her throat hot and swollen when she shot up in bed. Her eyes were glassy with fear as she desperately clutched the sheet around her shoulders.

Four-thirty. Too agitated to sleep, she got up, went to the kitchen, and poured a glass of milk. She drank it too fast, felt her stomach rebel and fled to the bathroom.

Finally exhausted, her entire body covered with a film of clammy perspiration, she went back to bed, pulled the sheet and the spread around her and once again fell into an uneasy sleep.

She dreamed of the man at the ferris wheel and the macabre carousel ride. She dreamed of Graham and Paul. This time Paul was staring at her with disappointment, as if she had failed him in some way. *"Betrayal . . . "* he said slowly, his eyes burning into hers. Over and over he repeated that one word . . . *"betrayal."*

At seven-thirty, she got up, feeling as if she'd never been in bed. Her head throbbed, her eyes were grainy and irritated, her stomach in spasms. She tried to eat some dry toast but threw most of it away.

After making her bed and doing a load of laundry, she made a half-hearted attempt to do some breathing exercises and scale warmups. Within a few minutes, however, she gave up. She was tired—incredibly tired.

An hour or so later, her head was assaulted by a mind-squeezing pressure. A crashing wave of pain was followed by a brief, heavily veiled image of a bald headed man walking toward her. His pale, icy stare loomed at her out of a mist. Someone was beside him . . . a tall man . . . a man with no face.

When the next pain hit her, she was bent over the kitchen sink, transplanting an African violet. It was busy work, something to occupy her hands, something that required little cooperation from her mind. The window above the sink was open, and she could hear the sound of whitecaps slapping rhythmically at the shore. The lake was choppy, the air close. She rinsed her hands, reached for a paper towel— and nearly slammed her head against the cabinet as another unexpected bolt of hot pain sent her groping for a chair.

Quickly, she put her head down, framing her face between her hands. A white blaze of light hurled itself forward in her mind and stopped, frozen for an instant like a halo around Paul's face. He was wearing the crewneck sweater and corduroy jeans he'd had on the last time she'd seen him. He had come to tell her about the unexpected trip, to say goodbye, to tell her . . . .

She waited for her memory of Paul to end there, as it always did. He would walk into her living room in the townhouse in Nashville wearing the funny, crooked little smile he always wore when he looked at her. He'd drop his hands gently to her shoulders, murmur "*angel,*" his private endearment for her, then disappear. Out of her vision, out of her life, even out of her memory.

From that point on, she would remember nothing until the memorial service. She would see herself, sitting at the front of the church . . . she would hear the organ sounding one of Paul's own praise anthems . . . she would be aware of quiet weeping, subdued whispers, the chokingly sweet, heavy scent of flowers . . . Leda beside her, clutching her hand, looking strong and heartbroken at the same time . . . Graham on the other side of her, his taut, angular face carved in suppressed mourning.

Always, there was that gap in her memory, like a deep, silent chasm separating those last few moments with Paul from the memorial service. Until now. Now a misty vignette began to inch its way past her memory's former stopping place. Once more she saw Paul's smile, heard him whisper again, "angel."

But this time there was more. The vision was shattered, like pieces that refused to come together. She felt him grip her forearms, saw the worry lines in his face, heard him say, "*If anything happens to me, don't trust anyone but my mother. Do you understand me, angel? She's the only one you can trust.*"

She sat upright, startled and frightened. What did it mean? Why would Paul have mentioned something happening to

126

him? What had he been trying to tell her? Dazed, she got up from the chair and began to pace the room.

This was the first time since the plane crash that a new scrap of memory had appeared. Why now? A sudden thought struck her and she stopped walking. *The medicine!*

She'd skipped last night's pill as Daniel had suggested. Could that possibly be responsible for the headaches, the baffling dreams, the bursts of memory? No. The thought was absurd.

But over the next two hours, three additional memory flashes invaded her mind. Each was more intense, more disturbing, than the other. By noon, she was frightened to the point of panic and decided to call Daniel. She was surprised at how quickly he responded to her question about the medication.

"No, I definitely don't think it's coincidence, Vali," he said bluntly. "If this is the first time you've experienced anything like this, I'd say we need to find out as much as we can about two things: The pills you've been taking, and whatever it is that's trying to fight its way out of your subconscious."

"But, Daniel—Graham wouldn't give me anything that would hurt me! And I have no idea what these . . . visions are."

Dan was quiet for a moment, then asked, "Do you think Leda could be of any help? That statement of Paul's you mentioned—about not trusting anyone but his mother— maybe Leda would be able to shed some light on that."

"I can't imagine how . . . "

"Vali, I think we ought to talk with Leda," Dan said firmly.

"I suppose . . . if you really think it's important . . . I could call Leda and see if she'd mind our driving in later today. It would have to be after four, though; she writes from early morning until three-thirty or four every day."

"Fine. Listen, would you like us to come over so you won't be alone?"

"Oh . . . no. I'm all right. But, Daniel—do you think Jennifer would drive, if we go to Leda's? I don't think I should, the way I feel . . . . "

"I'm sure she'll be glad to. We'll just come over about four unless I hear from you, all right?"

A few minutes after she hung up, David arrived.

She gave him a blank stare when she answered his knock at the door, then remembered they were to rehearse at one-thirty.

"Oh, David—I forgot! I'm sorry . . . I should have called you . . . I can't possibly sing today."

He walked inside without waiting to be asked. "What's wrong, princess? Are you ill? You look awful."

When she avoided his gaze and started to turn away from him, he caught her by the arm. "Vali? What is it?"

"I'm . . . not feeling well," she said evasively. "I hope you don't mind if we cancel today."

"Can I do anything? Do you want me to call Leda?"

She shook her head. "No—I'll be all right. It's just . . . a bad headache."

He touched her cheek, his eyes studying her relentlessly. "You're sure that's all?"

Vali finally looked at him, her breath catching in her throat when she saw the tenderness in his gaze. He touched the palm of his hand to the side of her face. "Vali . . . princess, what is it? What's the matter?"

When the phone rang, both of them jumped and turned toward it. Vali quickly crossed the room and lifted the receiver, glancing almost guiltily at David when she answered.

"Graham—hello." Feeling somewhat reassured by his strong, confident voice, Vali turned away from David's studying gaze.

"Are you all right, dear? Your voice sounds odd."

"I'm fine . . . fine," she answered quickly. "I've had a

headache most of the day, that's all."

"Probably your nerves. Vali, I've been doing some thinking about this idea you have of talking with Daniel Kaine," he said pragmatically, "and I really don't think it's wise. I talked with a friend of mine today who's quite well respected in his field—he's a psychologist, but he has an M.D. as well. If you really think you need counseling, he'll be glad to take you as a patient."

She took a deep breath. "I . . . Graham . . . I've already talked with Daniel."

His voice turned suddenly cold. "Wasn't that rather impetuous, Vali?"

"I—" She glanced at David, unnerved by his piercing stare.

Vali heard Graham's deep sigh and knew he was groping for patience. "And what was the outcome?" he asked tautly.

She hesitated, not wanting to anger him. Still, he *was* responsible for giving her the medicine.

He was furious when she told him about the pills. "What an *incredibly* irresponsible suggestion for him to make!" he exploded. "And you actually *listened* to him?"

"Graham, please . . . I have to do *something*."

"What does that mean?"

"You know . . . . " She felt a sudden surge of irritation with him. "*You're* the one who's always reminding me of how . . . fragile my emotions are."

There was a long silence. "I thought you trusted me," he finally said.

"I *do* trust you, Graham!" she assured him. "But I want to be . . . independent for once in my life. Can't you understand? I'll never be emotionally healthy as long as I have to depend on you or your mother to make my decisions for me."

His tone softened somewhat. "I *do* understand, Vali. But you simply must be patient with yourself. And," he said meaningfully, "you have to use good judgment. Now, then—tell me exactly what Kaine suggested during this . . . conversation, and how you've been feeling since."

He said little as she told him about her conversation with Daniel. Occasionally he muttered a short sound of agreement or disagreement. But at least he no longer sounded angry.

"Vali, as mild as that medication is—and I can assure you that it *is* mild—you can't just drop it all at once. Not without having some side effects. And if Kaine were as qualified as he'd like you to think, he'd know that."

"Graham . . . Daniel didn't try to mislead me. If anything, he was reluctant to even talk with me, he . . . . "

"Yes, yes—I'm sure," he interrupted. "However, the point is that he had no business giving you advice at all." He paused. "So the headaches and these . . . dreams started last night."

"Yes."

"And you think they may be related to the pill you *didn't* take." He made no attempt to hide his sarcasm.

"I . . . I don't know what to think."

"And you're going to see Mother later today?" Graham asked, his disapproval evident.

"Yes. Daniel thought she might be able to help." She hesitated a moment, then said guardedly, "Graham . . . are you sure you don't remember anything significant about the last time you were with Paul? You said the two of you talked . . . . "

"Vali, I've told you everything about that night," he said patiently. "Paul came out to the Center. We had coffee, we talked for a few minutes about our careers and your forthcoming marriage. That's all. We were together no more than half an hour before he left."

She drew in a long breath of disappointment, saying nothing. The heavy weight of exhaustion she'd felt earlier

130

settled over her again.

"I'll drive you in to Mother's later," Graham was saying. "If you don't mind, that is. I'd like to be there, just in case something should come up that upsets you."

He was so protective of her. *Occasionally too protective*, taunted a nasty little voice inside her head. She flushed guiltily. There really *was* something wrong with her if she resented a man like Graham wanting to take care of her.

"I'd like you to be there, Graham. I was going to ask Jennifer to drive us in, since I'm so shaky. But if you really want to . . . . "

"Of course, I want to. It'll give me a chance to see you, after all." Sounding somewhat mollified, he told her goodbye and hung up.

She took her time in replacing the receiver before turning back to David. He was slouched against the piano, studying her with a hard stare.

"What kind of pills has Graham been giving you, Vali?" he asked harshly.

Vali had suddenly had enough. Her nerves were raw, her head was hammering, and she simply couldn't face another involved explanation. "You obviously made it a point to listen to our conversation, David, so you shouldn't need any details," she snapped.

Something flared in his eyes—anger, she thought—but it quickly disappeared. Slowly, he pushed himself away from the piano and walked over to her, his gaze never leaving her face. "I'm sorry. I suppose I shouldn't have stayed. But you're right—I did hear the conversation. That's why I'm worried, princess."

When she saw the soft warmth in his eyes, she felt miserable that she'd been so short with him. "David . . . I didn't mean to snap at you. It's this headache . . . and I didn't sleep . . . I'm just on edge, I suppose."

"Vali . . . " Gently, he put his hand on her shoulder. "*Do*

131

you trust Graham? I know what you told him—but do you?"

"Of course, I do!" She raised her chin defiantly.

He searched her eyes with a steady, questioning gaze. "Are you in love with him?" he asked bluntly.

Surprised, she stammered, "I—you know I care for Graham . . . ."

"I asked if you're in love with him."

"You have no right, David . . . "

"And you haven't answered me, Vali."

Her eyes blazed. "It's none of your business."

She saw him swallow hard once, then again. As she watched, his expression gentled and his mouth softened to a sad, uncertain smile. "You're right. It's not."

Vali felt an unexpected sting of shame. "David . . . "

Slowly he lifted one hand, lightly grazed her cheek with his fingertips, then touched her hair. "I just want to see you happy, princess," he whispered, his eyes caressing her face. "You're so special, lovely Vali . . . so very, very special."

She felt tears burn her eyes, and she tried to turn away. He caught her by her shoulders, moving her gently but firmly around to face him. Her heart stopped when she saw the look on his face. He was smiling at her, not a happy smile but a wistful smile of regret that made her heart ache. For some inexplicable reason, she suddenly wanted to comfort him.

"David . . . "

She stopped breathing as he dipped his head to touch a feather light kiss onto her forehead. For one brief, tender moment, he circled her with his arms and gathered her carefully to him. Vali didn't know what to do, what to say. Awkwardly, she put her hands on his shoulders and stared up into his face.

"I'll go now, princess," he whispered. "Maybe you can get some rest. I'm sorry if I upset you. Forgive me?"

She nodded weakly. He slowly released her from his embrace, then turned to go. As Vali stood in silence and watched him leave, she squeezed her eyes tightly shut against the tears fighting to spill over. She did not understand the sweetness of emotion she had felt in his arms . . . nor the overwhelming sorrow she now felt in his absence.

But he had left something behind, something she knew she would cling to, just as she had savored the hope Daniel had given her yesterday when he'd told her she was "special . . . not so much because you're *you*—but because you're *His* . . . because you're a child of God."

David, too, had told her she was "special . . . so very, very special."

She wanted, with all her heart, to believe both of them.

14

The man answered the telephone reluctantly, listened, then muttered a grudging hello.

"So—did she talk to the blind man?" the voice at the other end of the line asked without preamble.

He hesitated, but not for long. "She talked to Kaine, yes."

"And?"

Again he paused before replying. "He . . . suggested that she skip the medication for a couple of days. To see how she would feel."

"And did she?"

He sighed. "Yes."

"With what consequences?"

"As I've already explained to you, if the block is not reinforced every forty-eight hours, control begins to fragment. At that point, it's quite possible for slices of memory to break through."

"Am I to assume that this . . . breakthrough . . . has begun?"

He cleared his throat and mumbled a short, "Yes."

"Is there any possibility of getting her back on the medication immediately?"

"Not likely," the man grated. "I think Kaine has made her suspicious of the pills. She'll probably resist taking any more, at least for now."

"I see. So, my friend . . . are you ready to be done with this entire business yet?"

Anticipating the question, he had already reviewed his choices. They were few and impractical. "Yes. Let's get it over with."

"Ah . . . finally, an objective attitude." More brusquely, the voice asked, "Do you know where she'll be tonight?"

"She and the Kaines are going to Sandusky," he replied thinly. "They're looking for additional clues."

The other man laughed shortly. "Fine. We'll provide them with a few they aren't expecting. Kaine and his wife are both going?"

"I think so."

"Good. This will be easier than we'd expected. We can take care of all of them at the same time. Now—it would be wise for you to absent yourself from them during the entire evening. Also, we'll need to be certain the singer drives her own car."

"She's not planning on driving at all. She was going to ask the Kaine woman . . . ."

"That's no problem. We'll simply put Kaine's automobile out of use for a bit."

"What are you planning to do?"

"You don't need to know that. Just rest assured that everything will be handled neatly and quietly. After tonight, there will be no loose ends to concern us."

"But shouldn't I be there? To make sure everything goes according to plan?"

"Not unless you want to die with the rest of them, my friend."

A muscle twitched rapidly at the side of his mouth. He hung up the phone and glanced around the room, dreary with late afternoon shadows. It had begun to rain a few minutes earlier, a light, monotonous splashing that worsened his already dismal mood.

He disliked this, hadn't wanted it. He'd thought the incident three years ago would be the end of it. Now there was to be more killing. Vali had to be eliminated, of course. He felt a twinge of regret but immediately curbed it. He'd known all along there was a chance she wouldn't be allowed to live. And it wasn't as if he were overly fond of her. Still, she'd become a part of his routine, a fixture in his life. Not that he'd miss her simpering. Actually, she was beginning to irritate him lately. The more trusting she became, the more she got on his nerves.

As for the Kaines, they deserved whatever they got. He had always detested people who meddled. And these two weren't even discreet about it. No loss there.

He uttered a sigh of exasperation, fingered his shirt collar, and glanced at the clock on the desk. Now that he'd accepted the inevitability of it, he was anxious for it to be finished. There had been one distracting aggravation after another lately. It would be good to have his routine in order again. *Order*, that was what he liked—and that was what he needed. He had always despised confusion, had thrived on neatness and exactness.

He smiled in anticipation. By tomorrow his life would once again be as he liked it. Neat. Well-ordered. And unencumbered.

15

"Jennifer, are you sure you don't mind driving?" Vali asked from the backseat. "Graham was all set to take us until he got that phone call from Ohio State. They wanted him there by five, so he had to leave right away," she explained, adjusting her seat belt.

"I don't mind at all, Vali, and it's no trouble for me to drive another Honda. I'm just burned up about the tires on my car, that's all," Jennifer said, glancing in the rearview mirror as she pulled out on Cleveland Road. "I hope you don't mind having Sunny in your car."

Vali looked over at the retriever, who was sitting up alertly on the seat beside her, staring out the window. "I wouldn't mind having Sunny with me anywhere," she answered with a smile. "Did you call the police about your tires?"

"We reported it as vandalism, but I'm afraid we were just wasting their time. My guess is that a couple of kids got cute and thought it would be macho to ruin my two front tires. There's no way the police can do anything about it now." She pushed the master switch on the power door lock and adjusted her side mirror. "The fellow at the service station said there's been a lot of vandalism up here."

Vali nodded. "He's right, I'm afraid. When can you get your car?"

"Tonight—any time after eight. I asked him to change the oil while he had it."

"I told you I'd do that when we get home," Dan said beside her. "You're just wasting money."

Rolling her eyes at Vali in the mirror, Jennifer answered, "I thought I'd save you the trouble this time."

"I *can* change the oil, Jennifer," he said somewhat testily.

"I know you can, Daniel. I don't doubt that for a minute."

"I change the oil in the station's Cherokee all the time."

She glanced at Vali again, lifting her eyebrows and grinning. "I know you do, Daniel."

"How much is he charging you?"

"How much? Ah . . . I don't know . . . I just asked him to change the oil when he replaced the tires."

"You didn't even ask him what he'd charge?" His expression was incredulous.

"Well . . . no."

He sighed.

"Next time I'll ask. Okay?"

"Are you sure those tires couldn't be fixed?"

"*Fixed?*" She looked over at him. "Daniel, they were in shreds! You examined them. No, they couldn't be fixed."

"Mm."

She glanced over at him. "Daniel . . . "

"Hm?"

"Are we having our first argument?"

"We had our first argument the day we met, Jennifer."

She thought about that. "Good. I wouldn't want to have our first one in front of Vali."

After a second, he grinned. "Was I making noises like a husband?"

"That's what it sounded like."

"I'm just practicing."

"Well, you can quit. You got it right the first time."

"Turn your windshield wipers on, Jennifer."

She looked at him again. "How did you know it was drizzling?"

He shrugged. "The way the tires sound on the highway."

She muttered to herself as she turned on the wipers.

"This road gets a little slippery when it's wet, Jennifer," Vali warned from the back seat.

"I'll watch it."

138

They drove along in silence for several minutes. Jennifer glanced in the rearview mirror every now and then, both for traffic and to watch Vali. She could tell by the way Vali was acting that she was still having "flashes," as Dan had called them. And she would guess, seeing her rub her temples, the headache was still with her, too.

She had a minor headache of her own, but she knew hers was weather related. It had been warm and humid all day and was now close enough to be uncomfortable. She fiddled with the air conditioning control and turned it up a notch.

"I bet we have a storm later," Dan said, breaking the silence.

"Daniel has radar," Jennifer explained to Vali soberly.

"It'll storm," he repeated with confidence.

"It probably will," his wife agreed grudgingly.

There was little traffic. Jennifer reached over to turn on the radio, keeping the volume soft so it wouldn't aggravate Vali's—or her own—headache. She played with the dial, stopping at a station that was giving the weather report.

"... *remember that a severe thunderstorm watch means conditions are favorable for heavy thunderstorms that may include dangerous lightning and strong winds. If you see a thunderstorm approaching, go to a place of safety....*"

"See," Daniel said smugly, "his radar picked up a storm, too."

Jennifer groaned playfully as she switched off the radio. Starting into a turn too fast, she gently tapped the brake. It seemed to her the brakes didn't grab, but she was afraid to apply any more pressure until she got out of the turn.

She bit her bottom lip, gripped the wheel, and as she came around the curve a startled cry of alarm broke from her throat.

Coming out of the turn, she found herself only a car's

139

length behind a small green farm truck plodding sluggishly along the road.

"What's wrong?" Dan asked sharply.

Jennifer was doing forty-five, the truck apparently no more than half that. She felt a beat of panic. Without answering Dan, she checked to see if it was clear to pass. A couple of cars were coming from the other direction, so she nosed back into her own lane, still applying enough pressure to the brake pedal to slow her speed. Nothing happened.

Her attention still riveted on the road, she said tightly, "Vali, the brake doesn't feel right—"

She glanced back to the truck. She was practically on top of it now. She floored the brake pedal. Nothing. The green truck was only feet away.

"The brakes are gone!" she choked out. "I've got to go around or hit him!"

She started to pull out, saw a semi coming toward her, and hesitated, trying to judge whether she could make it. Suddenly, as if out of nowhere, a big black sedan roared up beside her, forcing her back into her own lane and cutting off her outlet to pass. Relentlessly staying length-to-length with her, Jennifer was trapped.

She screamed. From behind her, Sunny started barking at the sedan. Vali leaned as far forward as her seat belt would allow, her eyes wide with fear. "He's doing that on purpose!" she cried out.

Desperately, Jennifer pumped the useless brake again. "We're going to hit—"

Dan reached over and began fumbling at the floor console. "Where's the emergency brake?"

Jennifer was anchored to the wheel, frozen speechless. Out of the corner of her left eye, though, she saw him. The bald man. He was staring straight ahead, watching the oncoming semi. For one brief instant, he turned his head in her direction. His icy, emotionless stare froze her blood.

Obviously agitated by the edge to Dan's voice, Sunny barked loudly, making Jennifer jump. Silencing Sunny with a sharp command, Dan shouted again, "*Jennifer*—the emergency brake!" Then he found and grabbed the lever before she could answer him.

At the last possible minute, the sedan roared ahead of Jennifer and passed the truck, weaving into his own lane just in time to avoid a head-on collision with the semi. He slowed immediately, forcing the farm truck behind him to cut his speed even more.

"Jennifer, I've got the brake! Go to the berm!" Dan yelled, squeezing the release button. "Hang on to the wheel—you'll skid!" he warned her as he raised the lever.

They were now close enough to the back of the truck to see the scratches on the panel. Her heart pounding furiously, Jennifer fought the wheel while Dan held the brake lever. Her grip on the steering wheel was white-knuckle rigid. She felt the rear wheels lock. The car skidded, lurched, skidded again. As much as possible she went with the skid, moving toward the berm of the road. The car started to fishtail, caught, pitched forward, then clung to the rough shoulder, finally stopping.

There was silence inside the car except for uneven, ragged breathing. Sunny whimpered once, and Vali moved to pat her reassuringly, though her hand trembled when she touched the dog's head.

Her eyes wide with shock, Jennifer watched the farm truck continue slowly on its way, the driver either mindlessly unaware or blissfully indifferent to the fact that he had very nearly been hit from behind. In front of him, the black sedan surged ahead, soon disappearing from view.

Jennifer sat shaking, her hands still locked on the steering wheel. Her chest felt as if someone had strapped a boulder on it. Her stomach began to riot, and her earlier headache asserted itself full force.

After a few seconds, Dan drew in a long, shaky breath, released the brake lever, and said, "You okay, honey?" His voice was thick and unsteady.

She had to wait until her teeth stopped clicking together to answer him. "All r-right," she said, still clutching the steering wheel as if she were afraid to let go of it.

"Vali?" Dan asked.

"I—y-yes. I'm . . . all right."

Dan reached over to touch Jennifer's hands. Very gently he pried one finger at a time from the wheel. "You did real good, honey," he said soothingly. "That was quite a landing."

Finally able to move, Jennifer looked over at him. "There was no brake," she said in a dazed voice. "Absolutely none."

Nodding, he squeezed her hand. "I know. But we're all right now, we're fine."

"I . . . couldn't stop . . . I couldn't . . . pass . . . I . . . . "

Quickly, Daniel released his seat belt and pulled her into his arms. "Easy, kid . . . easy. It's all right," he said softly, lightly patting and stroking her back to calm her down.

"It was the same man," Jennifer said in a low, tight voice against his shoulder. "He tried to kill us."

"What man? What are you talking about, honey?"

"Vali . . . did you see? The black car?"

"Yes," she said in a low, tremulous voice. "I saw."

Daniel started to say something, but Jennifer stopped him. "It was *him*, Daniel. It was the man I saw at Cedar Point—the same man who ran our bicycle off the road. He pulled up beside me so I couldn't go around and just . . . stayed there. I couldn't pass, I couldn't stop . . . he's trying to kill us, Daniel!" She stopped and caught her breath. "Who *is* he?" Her cry was muffled against his chest.

Dan's face creased to a worried frown as he tried to quiet her. "I don't know, honey. Listen . . . what we need to do

142

now is get some help. We can't drive without brakes."

Holding her with one arm, he pulled a handkerchief out of his back pocket.

"Is this white, honey?" He held out the handkerchief for her inspection.

Jennifer stared at it for a moment, then looked blankly at Dan. "White?"

"For a signal," he explained.

"Oh—yes. Yes, it's white."

"Okay, hang it out the window on your side," he told her, as the rain pattered softly on the car. "We'll just have to wait here until someone stops."

Almost half an hour passed before a deputy sheriff noticed the handkerchief and stopped to check on them. After a few questions, he radioed for a wrecker to pick up the car, then drove all of them back to Vali's cottage.

It was nearly nine o'clock that night before Dan could get any information from the garage in Huron where the wrecker had taken the car. Jennifer and Vali sat waiting on the sofa as he hung up the phone and turned toward them. Sunny's huge brown eyes watched him carefully from her place by his chair.

"The brake lines were cut," he said tersely.

"Cut?" Vali repeated in a shaky voice. "You mean someone . . . deliberately . . . "

"That's right. Someone deliberately took out your brakes."

The room was thick with tension for several minutes. Vali finally broke the silence. "There's something I probably should have told you before now. But at the time, I didn't think it was important."

She told them then about seeing the bald-headed man at the ferris wheel in Cedar Park—the same man who had been driving the black sedan today.

"So you saw him at the ferris wheel . . . before it broke

143

down," Dan said thoughtfully. "And Jennifer saw him again at the carousel before it . . . . " He didn't finish his sentence.

He was quiet for a long time. When he finally spoke, his voice was grave, his face as sober as Jennifer had ever seen it. "I think we need to face something here. I don't believe it's just coincidence that the tires on our car were sliced a few hours before Vali's brakes were tampered with. Any more than it's coincidence that this guy—whoever he is—keeps showing up every time something weird happens."

When neither of the women said anything, he lightly rapped his knuckles against the yellow countertop where he was standing, then went on. "It seems to me that someone wanted to make sure we drove Vali's car tonight instead of Jennifer's. And I'm afraid we can all figure out why."

He moved to the sink, felt for the cup he'd left on the counter earlier, then poured himself a cup of coffee.

"I'm so sorry for what I've done to the two of you," Vali said suddenly, her voice harsh with agitation. "For dragging you into this . . . nightmare. You could have been killed today—and apparently because of me!"

Dan turned back to the woman. "Forget that for now, Vali. But try to think of someone—anyone—who'd have a reason to hurt you. You say you don't recognize this man?"

She shook her head, then quickly said, "No. When I first saw him at Cedar Point, I thought he looked vaguely familiar. But today—no. I'm sure I've never met him before."

"What are we going to do, Daniel?" Jennifer asked.

He took a sip of coffee, then set the cup on the counter. Pushing his hands deep into his back pockets, he began digging at the floor with the toe of his shoe. "I think one thing we'd better do is talk to the police." Another thought struck him. "Vali . . . who else knew we were going to Sandusky tonight?"

"Who else?" Vali hesitated, then replied slowly, "Well . . . Graham, of course." She paused. "And David," she added softly.

"No one else?" Dan pressed.

"No."

"What about Leda? Did you call her?"

"I tried. But I got her answering machine—she uses it through the day when she's working. I left a message for her to call me back if there was any reason we shouldn't drive in tonight."

"What time did you call her?"

"It wasn't until later this afternoon—three-thirty, maybe."

"Then Jennifer's tires had already been cut by the time Leda would have known we were coming," he said, mostly to himself. He raked a hand down one side of his beard. "So . . . that leaves Graham—who's in Columbus—and David. They're the only ones who knew where we were going." Another thought struck him, and he asked, "Did both of them know why?"

Vali looked at him. "Why?"

"Did you tell both of them why we wanted to talk with Leda—because of that dream you had about Paul . . . what he said to you?"

Vali was silent for a long time, and Jennifer could tell she was struggling to remember.

Finally, she said, "No. I don't think I told either one of them. I *did* tell Graham everything else, though—about the headaches, the memory flashes . . . everything. And David was here, at the cottage, when I talked to Graham on the phone. I'm sure he heard the whole conversation. But no," she said again, "I'm almost positive I didn't say anything about Leda, except that we thought she might be able to remember something that would help."

As Jennifer watched, Vali's expression changed from

145

puzzlement to denial, then to something bordering on anger. "Graham was in Columbus," she said slowly. "So only David . . ."

Daniel put up a restraining hand. "Vali . . . I don't think we ought to jump to any conclusions. I *do* think it would be a good idea to call the police, though."

Vali remained silent until she got up and walked across the room toward the window. "I suppose you're right," she finally said in a soft voice, her back to them. "But if you don't mind, I'd like to have a little time. For one thing, I should call Leda and explain what happened. She'll be worried when we don't show up. And I need to . . . get myself together."

Dan nodded and started to move toward the door. Sunny got up and followed him. "Jennifer and I will go back to our place, get cleaned up a little and then come back over here, if you want."

Jennifer walked over and put her hand on Vali's shoulder. "Maybe you could rest for a little bit, too. You look awfully tired, Vali."

"I . . . yes, I am," she admitted, turning around from the window.

"Vali . . . " Dan paused, then said, "I don't think you should let anyone in—or talk with anyone—while you're here alone. No one but Leda. Until we know for sure what's going on."

She nodded numbly, her head down.

Jennifer looked at her with concern, then went to Dan, putting her hand on his arm. Turning to Vali, she gave her one more worried glance. "We'll be back soon, Vali."

Vali looked up, blinked a couple of times and finally managed a weak smile. "Yes. All right. I'll . . . be here."

It was raining steadily when they walked outside. Neither of them had a raincoat or jacket, so they walked as fast as they could. Tightening her grasp on Dan's arm as they hurried to their cottage, Jennifer asked, "Daniel, do you think David

146

could be . . . . " She left her question unfinished.

Dan shook his head. "I don't know, honey. The only thing I'm reasonably sure of right now is that someone wants Vali out of the way." He hesitated, then added, "And it's beginning to look as if they've got the same thing in mind for us, too."

Jennifer shivered but said nothing. She glanced nervously around at the dark, deserted beach, huddled closer to Dan and started to walk even faster.

16

A few minutes after Daniel and Jennifer left, Vali called Leda. Not wanting to worry her unnecessarily, she told her only that they'd had car trouble and wouldn't be in tonight. She knew things were coming to a head and that she'd eventually have to tell Leda the truth. But not, she reminded herself cynically, until she knew what the truth was.

After she hung up, she threw on a lightweight rain jacket and hurried out the door.

She suspected the rain now falling was only the prelude to a coming storm. The lake was stirring and heaving with the force of a gathering wind; the night air was close and thick with the smell of sand and decaying fish.

Indifferent to the rain, she half-ran the distance from her cottage to David's. As she jogged across the beach, she inwardly shrank from the uneasy feeling of guilt simmering at the back of her mind. If Daniel and Jennifer had been aware of her intention to see David alone, they undoubtedly would have tried to stop her. She knew their concern for her welfare was genuine—and apparently justified, considering the bizarre, frightening events of the past few days.

She couldn't explain even to herself why she felt the need to confront David alone—before the police were called, before he had a chance to cover his tracks. Perhaps it was the hurt, the raw pain, of his deceit.

Without knowing—or caring—what she might accomplish, Vali simply felt driven to face him, to force him to tell her the truth. She had to know why. Behind all this madness and treachery, there had to be a reason. The willful, calculated campaign of deception on his part, just when she was beginning to realize how much she cared for him, was very nearly the stroke that could put her over the edge emotionally. Before David had the opportunity to throw up some kind of a smoke screen, she intended to shock him into the truth.

There wasn't much time if she hoped to get back before Daniel and Jennifer returned. She resolutely tried to ignore the sting of warning that she might be placing herself in extreme jeopardy. If what she suspected about David was true, going to him alone would give him the opportunity to finish the aborted attempt on her life.

Somehow, though, it no longer mattered. Even if it meant losing her life, she had to know the truth. Besides, she had already reasoned that it might take Jennifer and Daniel out of danger if she could divert the focus of David's attention.

She hurried onto the porch to get out of the rain but stopped with her hand poised to knock. Almost breathless, she stood there, trying to force her tumultuous emotions under control as she listened to the music. He was playing a Faure nocturne, which surprised her; she had never thought of David playing anything but his own music. As she might have guessed, he played it expertly.

Vali had seen enough storms on the lake to sense that David's interpretation of the music was like the night itself— deceptively tranquil, but soon to build to a brilliant storm of passionate, thundering force. Even as angry and bewildered as she was, she found herself caught up in his artistry and mastery of the keyboard. Only when the music stopped was she finally able to knock.

When he opened the door, his eyes widened with surprise. It occurred to Vali that he looked unusually tired and somewhat disheveled. His hair was carelessly tossed, his shirt not quite as neatly tucked in as usual. Fine lines of fatigue bracketed his mouth.

Did she imagine that his eyes brightened as he stared at

her? "What are you doing out in this, princess?" Opening the door wider, he motioned her inside, lightly brushing her shoulder with his hand as she walked past him.

She flinched at his touch and avoided his gaze as she walked to the middle of the living room. Stopping a few inches away from the piano, she turned to face him.

He followed her with a puzzled look. "Something wrong?"

Ignoring his attempt to take her jacket, she threw it over a nearby chair.

For a long moment Vali could do nothing but stare at him, clenching her hands tightly at her sides. "You look surprised to see me," she finally said, a note of challenge in her voice.

"Surprised but pleased," he replied uncertainly. "Want some coffee?"

"No, I don't want any coffee, David," she answered flatly. "I want the truth."

He inclined his head, lifting his brows in a question. "The truth?"

Vali swallowed determinedly against the knot of unhappiness in her throat, suddenly knowing this was going to be even more difficult than she'd thought. She concentrated on holding herself together. Both physically and emotionally, she was stretched to the limit. Without warning, her head began to pound again, and she desperately hoped she wouldn't be sick.

He moved a little closer to her. "Vali? Why don't you sit down, princess? You look . . . ill."

"I'm sure I look better than you expected, though—right, David?"

He frowned. "What are you talking about?"

"I think you know exactly what I'm talking about," she said coldly, furious at his composure.

He shook his head. "Did I miss something?" He ventured a

smile and reached for her hand. "Hey, princess . . . I can see you're upset with me. But don't I at least get to know why?"

She recoiled from his touch, inching backward a few steps. "Why did you do it, David?"

"Do *what?*" He exchanged his smile for a bewildered frown. "Look, I don't know what's happening here, but I can't very well apologize when I don't even know what I've done, now can I?"

She stared at him with disbelief, feeling the blood in her veins begin to boil. "I'm curious, David," she said tightly, "how do you go about apologizing for trying to kill someone?"

His mouth dropped open. "*What?*" The startled whisper made the word sound strangely macabre.

"Oh, *stop* it!" she cried. The pounding at the back of her head accelerated. For an instant she was afraid she was going to pass out. She pulled in a deep breath, trying to steady herself. "You should have thought your plan through a little more carefully, David. Oh, it probably would have worked if *I* had been driving. But Jennifer's reflexes are much quicker than mine."

He closed the distance between them with two sweeping steps, grasping her by the shoulders. Anger sparked briefly in his eyes, then ebbed as he stared down into her ashen face.

"You obviously think I know what you're talking about," he rasped. "But I swear to you, I don't. Vali—tell me what's wrong."

As limp as a ragdoll under his hands, she was surprised to realize she felt no fear. Only disillusionment. And a terrible sense of betrayal.

Betrayal. The thought acted like a trigger, exploding Paul's face upon the canvas of her mind again. His hands had also gripped her shoulders that night, and his face had

151

been livid with anger. *Betrayal...*

She felt herself begin to sag. David caught her, led her across the room. She fought him, but he managed to push her down onto the couch. His whisper-voice sounded distant, detached... she felt the blackness closing in, the strumming in her head racing faster and faster. She squeezed her head between her hands with a soft moan.

"Vali... princess... what is it? Are you ill?" When he coaxed her head onto his shoulder, she was too weak to protest.

She started to cry, silently railing at herself for being so pathetically helpless. Another wall of pain engulfed her, seizing her with such an excruciating agony she stopped crying and gasped for relief.

"Vali, I'm going to get a doctor. Here, lean back. Lean back and close your eyes while I call a doctor."

"You tried to kill me ...all of us ... and now you're going to call a doctor?" She shot an unfocused, dazed look at him, trying unsuccessfully to twist away.

"Kill you—" He gaped at her, wide-eyed. "*Kill* you? What in the name of heaven are you talking about?" He dropped his hands and jumped to his feet, staring down at her with an expression that looked almost like fear.

For an instant, Vali wondered if she could have possibly been wrong. He looked so—stricken, so dumbfounded. Quickly, she gave herself a mental shake. She wasn't mistaken ... it couldn't have been anyone else but David.

She pushed herself up off the couch, fighting the pain in her head, the crazy zigzags of color and shattered pictures flailing at her. "*Why*, David? What are you doing here? What do you want? What's so important to you that you'd try to kill three people?"

He shook his head slowly back and forth as if he were trying to clear it. "Vali—you've got to believe me. I haven't tried to kill anyone. I don't know what you're talking about, I

152

tell you! I don't *know!*"

Suddenly, she wished with all her heart she could believe him. Another flash went off inside her head, this time an unwelcome glimmer of insight: She didn't *want* it to be David. He was too . . . important to her. She looked away from him, trying to avoid his searching eyes. *Whether I want to believe it or not, he tried to kill me today. I mustn't forget that, I don't dare forget it.*

Without trying to touch her, David lifted both hands in a palms-up gesture of supplication. "Just . . . tell me," he whispered. "Tell me what it is I'm supposed to have done, princess. Please."

Anger flooded her again. "Why, David? Why should I tell you what you already know?" She took a step toward him, then stopped, struck by the thought that she was alone with this man, that he had tried unsuccessfully to kill her once, and that there was nothing to stop him from trying it again. Why, then, didn't she feel threatened?

She heard her own voice as if coming out of a thick fog. "Did you know about the farm truck, David? Did you hire the driver? Or is it just the psychopath in the black sedan who works for you?"

She hurled her words at him like stones, giving him a furious, detailed account of the entire incident. She told him about the truck, the useless brakes, the slick highway, the black sedan, its driver. She told him everything she was sure he already knew, unaware that by the time she had finished her passionate recital she was sobbing desperately.

"Vali . . . princess . . . "

Suddenly she realized that he was holding her again, clasping her forearms, his gaze raking her face.

"Vali, did you say the brakes were cut?"

She raised her head, studying him with a dull, leaden stare. "You know they were," she said woodenly. "You know."

He winced, and she saw a small muscle by his heavy left

eye jerk spasmodically. Dimly, she wondered why he looked so . . . frightened.

"You think I did that, Vali? Do you really think I'd do anything to hurt you?"

She tried to look away from him, but he wouldn't let her. He caught her chin with his hand and forced her to meet his gaze.

"Vali, listen to me. *Listen!*" he demanded when she tried to twist free. His face looked lined and grim. "It wasn't me, Vali. I would never do anything to hurt you. Don't you know that by now? I *couldn't.*"

How could he lie so convincingly, even now? She felt the rivers her tears were making as they splashed down her face. She tried to free her hands to wipe her eyes, but he held her. *Oh, David . . . why . . . why did it have to be you?*

"Vali—" There was a new urgency in his whisper. "*Please* listen to me. Whose car was Jennifer driving—her own or yours?"

She looked at him blankly. "Mine."

"Why? Why didn't she drive her own car?"

Again she hesitated before answering him. "Her tires— someone slashed her tires."

His eyes narrowed. "Who else knew you were going to Sandusky tonight?"

Her throat was tight, her mouth dry. Her heart was a crazy thing, racing as if it were about to fly out of her chest, then slowing as though it would stop any second. "Who else?"

"Yes. It's important. Did anyone besides me—and Graham—know what you were planning to do?"

She thought. "No. Just you," she answered with an accusing look. "And Graham." She shook her head firmly. "No one else."

He swallowed hard, still holding onto her. Moistening his lips, he squeezed his eyes shut, then opened them and said,

"It wasn't me, Vali. I *swear* to you—it wasn't me."

She continued to stare up at him, flushed with anger and disbelief. "Then . . . who?"

He pulled in a ragged, shallow breath. "Graham."

She tried to yank herself free. Crying out in frustration when he continued to hold her firmly, she wrenched her arms, straining and tugging in a desperate frenzy.

"No! Don't you *dare* blame him for what you did! Don't you dare!"

David clutched her shoulders, not tightly enough to hurt her, but firmly enough to keep her from breaking away from him. "It was Graham." His steady, unwavering gaze held her eyes.

Suddenly she remembered. "Graham went to Columbus!"

He shook his head. "No. He may have told you that, but he didn't go." David stopped, searching her eyes. "You have to believe me, Vali. Graham is the one responsible."

She stared at him, her gaze wounded and stunned.

David took her hand and began to lead her toward the couch. "Let's sit down . . . ."

His action broke her paralysis. Seizing her chance, Vali jerked her hand from his and ran to the door. But he easily outdistanced her and blocked the door with his body. "You can't go. You're not safe anywhere but here now."

She choked off a sound of disgust, and backed away from him. "That's a joke!"

"Vali . . . princess . . . "

"Don't call me that!"

"I wouldn't hurt you . . . "

" . . . you tried to kill me . . . "

"Never . . . I would never hurt you . . . "

" . . . you would have killed me . . . "

"No. I love you . . . "

She closed her eyes. Then opened them. "What did you say?"

155

"I love you," he said again, his whisper broken and hoarse. "I could never hurt you. You're my heart, my life."

Her voice shook. "You're lying."

"Come here, Vali." He extended one hand to her.

She shook her head furiously.

His hand touched hers. "Vali . . . come here. I have something to tell you."

He pressed her fingers with his, then covered her slender hand with his own large one, tugging her gently to him. Slowly, carefully, he drew her into the circle of his arms.

She felt the trembling of his hands, heard him utter a deep, ragged sigh. "My love . . . " His lips brushed her brow with infinite tenderness. "It's true I'm not what you think."

She stiffened.

He tightened his embrace and pressed his lips against her temple. "Vali . . . I'm not . . . David Nathan Keye. I'm . . . Paul."

He touched his cheek to hers and said again, "I'm Paul . . . *angel.*"

156

17

The world stopped. Her legs buckled under her. She couldn't breathe, couldn't move, couldn't speak. She could only tremble in his arms, in the arms of this stranger, this madman who was intent upon taking her last shred of sanity.

His arms tightened around her, supporting her. "It's true, Vali."

He tipped up her chin so she'd have to look at him. Weakly, she shook her head. "You're insane," she choked out.

"No."

She stared up at him in horror through glazed, tortured eyes. "How dare you . . . " she whispered. "How dare you say that to me?"

With deliberate care, he put her slightly away from him, clasping her shoulders only firmly enough to keep her from pulling free. His eyes burned into hers, willing her to listen to him. "I can prove what I'm saying, Vali. I know I don't look like myself—" He freed one hand to touch his hair, then his beard. "Everything is different. But not this." He touched his heart. "This is the same. It still belongs to you, angel."

It was his use of the endearment again—Paul's endearment—that shattered what little control she had left. She cried out once, then again. He pulled her to him, holding her, soothing her, muffling the sound of her incoherent, heartrending weeping in the hollow of his shoulder.

He began to move her, half-carrying her, toward the couch. "Here, angel, sit down," he whispered, touching his lips to her windblown hair. "Sit here with me. I'm sorry . . . I'm so sorry I did this to you. I know it's awful for you. Here, sit close to me . . . I'll tell you everything . . . I'll tell you the truth now."

She let him pull her down beside him on the couch. He continued to hold her, gently but securely within his arms, stroking her hair. He touched her face. "I don't know where to start. There's so much . . . . "

Tears streamed down her face. Her mind was spinning, her head throbbing. Then her eyes narrowed, and she drew away from him as she remembered something else. "You can't be Paul! I knew you were lying," she said, her words spilling out in a breathless rush. "Your eyes—"

He held up an unsteady hand. "Wait," he said. He turned away for a moment. When he again faced her, he extended his hand, palm upward. He was holding two tinted contact lenses.

A stunned whimper escaped her throat when she looked into his eyes, still gray but lighter now. Pressing her fingertips against her mouth, she stared at him with a mixture of fear and disbelief.

He lifted a hand to gently smooth a springy wave of hair away from her temple. His touch was achingly tender when he brushed the tip of his index finger over her ear. "Little seashells," he whispered. "Remember? I always teased you that your ears looked like little seashells."

She shuddered on a choked, incredulous sob.

"Remember the day we spent at Radnor Lake?" His face softened to a smile that was both sad and reflective. "You took off your sandals so you could run free. But you sprained your ankle and we ended up in the emergency room. Remember the nurse who admitted you? Her name was 'Sam.' When she found out who we were, the only thing she was interested in was whether or not we knew Amy Grant." He threaded his fingers through her hair, then watched, fascinated, as the russet waves sifted slowly through his fingers and fell lightly back into place.

158

Tears began to spill from her eyes again as she stared at him, remembering a man of incredible gentleness, a man whose love had always been sweet and steady and dependable. She squeezed her eyes shut, her narrow shoulders heaving with the force of her silent weeping and tumultuous emotions.

He wrapped her more snugly in his arms. "Don't cry, angel . . . don't cry anymore," he whispered against her lips just before he touched them with his own in a kiss that told her the truth as nothing else could have.

She dragged his name out of her heart as if it were the first time she'd ever said it. *"Paul . . ."*

"Ah, what a feeling, hearing you say my name again, holding you again . . . ."

Still crying, she searched his face, drinking in every line, every plane of it as if seeking a familiar landmark. "Your eye," she choked out.

He closed his heavy left eye under her gentle touch. "The plane crash, angel. My face was . . . destroyed. They had to give me a new one. A few weeks after the surgery, they noticed my eye was drooping a little. I told them to leave it. I wasn't about to start over."

She put her hand on his throat. "Your voice . . ."

"My voice box was crushed. This is permanent, I'm afraid."

Her face wilted with sadness. "Your beautiful voice . . ."

Quickly he pressed his lips against the palm of her hand. "It doesn't matter. After everything else that's happened, it's not important. As long as I can still tell you I love you, that's enough."

Another thought struck her as she ran her hands over his shoulders. "You're so thin."

He shrugged and managed a wobbly grin. "Don't you remember? I don't eat when I don't work. And I wasn't able to work for months."

Choking on her tears, she examined his face with her hands much as Daniel had a few days before, slowly shaking her head from side to side in wonder. "But they said you were dead—the papers, the television—everyone told me you were dead."

He grabbed her hands, framed them with his own, brushed his lips over her knuckles. "You don't know how I hated that... but it had to be that way." Suddenly he stopped. Raising his face from her hands, he searched her eyes. "Angel, don't you remember anything... about that last day we were together? The day I came to see you in Nashville, before I went to Washington?"

"Remember?" She shook her head. "No... just... you coming into my apartment. You said you couldn't stay long, that you had to leave for Washington... you kissed me...."

He nodded, a sad smile hovering about his mouth. "Nothing else?"

"No. I don't remember anything after that until...."

"The plane crash?"

"Yes," she whispered, then moved her hands to clutch his shoulders. "I wanted to die, too!" she grated harshly, her eyes burning with a feverish glint. "I *prayed* to die!"

"Oh, angel... I'm so sorry you had to go through that." His eyes misted as he studied her face.

Suddenly she drew back from him, a fresh wave of anger coursing through her. "How could you do that to me? How could you let me believe you were dead when you were alive? And for *three years!*"

A violent trembling racked her body, and she hugged her arms rigidly against herself. "Do you know what happened to me? I almost lost my mind! I was in a sanitarium for months, I was...." The words died in her throat.

He started to reach for her again, then let his hands drop away. "I know... I *do* know, Vali. But there was nothing I

160

could do. You see, while you were going through *your* nightmare, I was going through one of my own. Almost two years of plastic surgery, one operation after another—skin grafts, bone reconstruction, physical therapy. Then, when they finally got me to the point where I didn't look like some kind of monster out of a late-night TV show, they started on the psychological conditioning—turning me into a new person, giving me a whole new identity."

Now he reached for her hands, and she limply allowed him to enfold them in his. "What you have to understand, angel, is that I *would* have been a dead man if I'd come back into your life as Paul Alexander. For months after the plane crash, I didn't know what you'd been told. By the time I found out, everything had been set in motion and there was no going back. They made it clear that my life—and probably yours—depended on my carrying this off . . . ."

"They? Who is *they*?" she cried in frustration, yanking her hands away from him. "And carry *what* off? *Who* put you through the surgery? And where were you all that time . . . when I thought you were dead? I still don't understand how you could have let me go on believing that."

"It was the only way, Vali. You'll understand when I explain the whole story . . . "

" . . . and when you finally *do* come back into my life, you don't look like yourself or talk like yourself or even *act* like yourself! You carry on this horrible . . . masquerade! You let me believe you're someone else, you lie to me—" She pressed the fingertips of both hands hard against her temples. "*Why*? Why didn't you just tell me the truth?"

He put his hands on her shoulders and pulled her close, staring intently into her eyes. "I couldn't. Telling you who I was would only have placed you in jeopardy along with me."

He continued to rake his gaze over her face as if he couldn't get enough of the sight of her. "Vali . . . after the

161

plane crash . . . I was unconscious for days, then out of my head for weeks. I was totally irrational—delirious with pain. I was . . . burned . . . horribly. Third degree burns over much of my body. You can't imagine the pain—"

He shook his head as if to banish the memory. "You say you prayed to die? Well, angel, I *begged* to die!"

Suddenly he seemed to realize he might be hurting her with the strength of his grip. He dropped his hands away, no longer touching her. "All that time," he said, less agitated now, "all that time they were rebuilding me, restoring me . . . and drilling me, coaching me, pounding at me to make me realize that this was the only way I'd ever be able to come back into your life. If I were to . . . live again, it had to be as a new man. So I could come back to you and protect you from Graham. And, at the same time, help them get enough evidence to stop him."

The impact of his words stunned her into silence. When she finally tried to speak, she felt as if her mouth were paralyzed. "Protect me . . . from Graham? What do you mean?"

He studied her for a moment with a measuring gaze. "Vali, the plane crash that supposedly killed me was no accident. The engines were sabotaged. Graham . . . and the people he works for . . . were responsible."

She felt a cold shroud wrap itself around her shoulders. She began to shiver, at first imperceptibly, then harder. "Graham?" She shook her head in denial. "No. Graham wouldn't hurt anyone, especially not you. He loved you; he admired you; he wouldn't—"

"Graham is totally incapable of loving anyone or anything," Paul rasped, his eyes blazing. "Graham cares about nothing but his experiments, his work." He got up and began pacing the floor in front of her, his steps uneven and faltering.

Vali sat unmoving for the next several minutes, mutely

listening as he told her about a conspiracy of terror too incredible, too fantastic, to be anything less than the truth. As he spoke, his words began to act as probes, setting into place the missing pieces of the puzzle her mind had been unable to solve for years.

"The last day of my vacation that summer—the day before I was to come back to Nashville—I spent most of it with Mother, then went over to Woodson Institute. Graham was their top research man before he built the Center, remember? It was late—eight, maybe nine o'clock—but it wasn't unusual for him to work that late. Since I planned to leave early the next morning, I decided to go over to the lab and tell him goodbye."

He stopped walking, reached in his shirt pocket for a stick of gum and tucked it in his mouth.

Irrelevantly, Vali said, "You never used to chew gum."

"New habit for the new me," he said dryly. He winked at her, and she caught her breath. The wink was an old habit, one that had always made her feel . . . special.

"Anyway," he continued, "I started into the lab, but I heard voices so I waited in the adjoining office. The door was ajar just enough for me to overhear the conversation going on inside. What I heard froze my blood. I sat there and listened to my own brother commit treason." He shook his head as if he still found it impossible to believe.

"*Treason?*" She gaped at him.

He nodded. "Oh, I couldn't hear everything. But I heard enough to find out that Graham had apparently been concealing the results of some of his experiments from the Woodson people and selling—or trading—them to someone else. Someone," he said slowly and meaningfully, "not affiliated with our scientific community. Someone," he added, "who wasn't even an American. The man who walked out of the lab with Graham that night had an accent that even *I* recognized as east European."

163

"What kind of experiments?" Vali hugged her arms to herself, shaking her head slowly in bewilderment. "David—" she stopped, stared at him for a moment, then corrected herself. "*Paul*, this sounds like something out of a science fiction novel."

He smiled weakly and dropped down beside her on the couch. "Doesn't it? That's what I thought, too, at the time."

He sighed and took one of her hands in his. "Graham's specialty for years has been in the field of psychotropic drugs."

"Psychotropic? What's that?"

"Any drug that affects the mental processes. Marijuana, hashish, hallucinogens. But Graham has gone far beyond all those with his research. He's developed some real state-of-the-art stuff—consciousness altering, memory blocking, redirection of the thought processes, and a lot more. He worked at top-secret level with Woodson for years to develop ideas for our own government, but Graham has always been too ambitious to remain just another research man."

He paused and looked down at her hand in his for a moment, studying it with thoughtful tenderness. "Anyway," he said, going back to his explanation, "what I heard that night at the lab made it obvious that Graham had a ... partner who was going to finance his experiments in exchange for Graham furnishing a foreign government some experimental drugs and copies of his journal entries regarding those drugs. There was to be a research center, plenty of money—a scientist's dream." He raised his eyes to her. "The present Alexander Center."

"You said you were there when they came out of the lab . . . ."

He nodded. "That was my first mistake."

"What do you mean?"

He uttered a short, voiceless laugh. "I've never been too

164

good at keeping my mouth shut—I'm sure you remember—"

She glanced down at her lap, and for the first time since she'd entered the house, a hint of a smile played at her lips. "Yes. I remember."

"I lit into Graham as soon as the other guy was out the door . . . and told him just exactly what I thought of him and what I was going to do about it. Like a fool, I issued an ultimatum—told him to bring his entire obscene operation to a screeching halt—or I would go to Uncle Kevin."

"Uncle Kevin?"

"One of my dad's best friends. We always called him 'Uncle Kevin' when we were kids. He's been with the CIA for years. In the back of my mind, I suppose I thought I could either shame or scare Graham into cleaning up his act."

"Oh, Paul . . ."

He gave her a crooked grin. "I know—purely stupid. But I was *furious*. Not only because he was betraying his country, but as much because of the kind of poison he was fooling around with. To me, this mind-control stuff is immoral. And scary. Graham used to dribble this garbage about the way scientists would eventually bring an end to all wars, that ultimately it would be the scientists who would establish universal peace by controlling the entire human race with chemicals." He stopped, combed his hair with his fingers, and sighed.

"What did he say when you confronted him?"

"Oh, he was cool. Graham is *always* cool, you know. He looked at me with one of those aristocratic frowns of his, called me ignorant, and then proceeded to explain how he had been doing some research for a private business in Europe. It was a slick comeback, but I knew him too well— well enough to know he was lying. Graham's an uncanny liar, but he's never been too successful at it with me."

He twisted his mouth with self-disgust. "Then I made my second mistake. I let him know I didn't believe anything he'd said and went charging out of the lab like some kind of college hero."

He stopped for a moment when a strong sweep of wind rattled the living room windows. He waited until the noise from a sudden roll of thunderclaps subsided before continuing.

"So . . . I carried out my threat and went to Washington, stopping off in Nashville to see you. Once Kevin heard my story, he arranged for an Agency pilot to fly me back to Sandusky on a private prop job. But at the last minute, he decided to go with me. I thought he was going home with me to try and talk some sense into Graham. I found out later that he had a pretty good idea even then who Graham was dealing with and was concerned about my safety."

He leaned forward and propped his elbows on his knees, framing his face with both hands in a gesture of fatigue. "What I hadn't counted on, of course, was that Graham's contacts had found out about my trip to Washington."

"There were three of you on the plane?" Vali asked with surprise. "All the news stories said it was only you and the pilot."

He nodded. "That was deliberate. What actually happened was that the pilot got a Mayday out on a scrambled frequency before we went down. He was killed, but an Agency helicopter picked up Kevin and me within minutes after the crash. Kevin wasn't too badly hurt. I was unconscious, and badly burned." He tapped the knee of his right leg. "My leg was caught under the seat, and they had trouble pulling me free. They got me out just before the plane went up. On the chance that the crash had been rigged, Kevin and the pilot of the helicopter made an on-the-spot decision to report me as dead and to conceal the fact that Kevin had been with me . . . so Graham and his friends would think they had nothing to worry about. The plane was almost completely destroyed by fire, so no remains could be identified . . . . " He shrugged, leaving the rest unsaid.

"But how could they be sure that it was sabotage—that the plane didn't simply crash?" Vali asked him.

When he raised his head to look at her, she saw the undisguised anguish in his eyes. "They weren't sure, not a hundred percent. Not until they got it on tape, thanks to a high-tech listening device that was installed in Graham's condo. Installed, incidentally," he told her with a small, grim smile, "by the same people who have been buying his experimental drugs and journals."

He nodded his head when she stared at him with surprise. "Right. His pals didn't trust him either. They bugged his lab, his condominium—" he paused and leveled an assessing look at her—"and your phone."

Her face contorted with astonished anger. "*My* phone?"

"Don't get too upset, angel," he told her. "It turned out to be an advantage for us. One of Kevin's agents traced Graham's contact and found out where he's staying. He spent a very productive hour in the guy's apartment the other night while this character and Graham were together at the Center. He copied a few tapes that turned out to be very interesting. One of which," he said tautly, "includes a conversation about a certain airplane crash." He paused, then added, "On one of the later tapes, there was a discussion about the most effective way to . . . take care of you."

Vali felt a knot of fear tighten in her stomach at the significance of his words.

"The main reason for me being here was to keep an eye on you, to keep tabs on what was going on in your life and Graham's while the Agency did their job. They knew I wouldn't last a day if I came back as Paul Alexander. Not only could I incriminate Graham, but I could also point the finger at his contact. Without an eyewitness, Graham probably couldn't have been indicted. With my input, there's a good chance of making the charges stick."

167

"Oh, Paul, you'll have to testify against your own brother?"

"There's no other way to stop him, Vali."

He said nothing more for a moment, then gave her a shaky smile. "What complicated things for me was finding out that you didn't remember anything I'd told you that day in Nashville before I left for Washington."

At her puzzled frown, he drew in a deep breath and explained. "Vali . . . I told you everything I knew. What I'd seen, what I'd heard—even what Graham's contact looked like. I told you where I was going—and why."

He lowered his head to his hands for a moment, rubbed his face wearily, then looked up at her. "When I stopped to see you, you got upset with me because I'd already been gone for several days, and there I was, leaving again. I knew I shouldn't say anything, but I was upset, worried—and I just . . . spilled it. The words were no more out of my mouth than I wanted to eat them. Later, when I found out that you apparently didn't remember anything I'd told you, I got positively paranoid about what would happen if you ever *did* remember. I had to live with the fear that if they found out you knew, they might snuff you out like one of Graham's lab animals. I'm sure he's always felt threatened by you—just because there was that chance you *might* remember something."

She was stunned. "But . . . why can't I remember—" Suddenly she realized that she *had* been remembering. Pieces. Fragments. Scraps of memory had been floating in and out of her mind all day. She simply hadn't been able to fit them together. Paul's face . . . his anger . . . that anger had been directed at Graham, not at her. *Betrayal* . . . he'd used that word when he told her what Graham had done. And the man, the bald man . . . Paul had described him to her . . . that's why he had looked familiar.

His harsh whisper broke into her thoughts. "Up until now, I just thought it was the shock of the plane crash—that it had done something to your memory." His mouth thinned to a hard, angry line. "But after overhearing your conversation with Graham today, I've got a hunch those little pills he's been giving you have something in them besides a tranquilizer."

Wide-eyed, she touched her fingers to her lips. "You think Graham has deliberately . . . "

"Blocked your memory," he finished for her. "You bet I do."

Suddenly another thought struck her. "*Leda!* She doesn't know? That you're . . . alive?"

He met her gaze. "No. That's been tough. You know how sharp she is. I was really squirming the night of your birthday party."

At her questioning frown, he said, "The strawberries, remember? She zeroed in on me with one of her eagle-eyed stares when I said I couldn't eat them. For a minute, I thought she suspected something."

He gave her a rueful smile. "And when I sat down to play my piano again—" He shook his head. "I'd been crazy to get to that keyboard every time she had us over for an evening. Not being able to touch my own piano . . . was almost as difficult as not being able to touch you." The expression of love and longing he turned on her brought tears to her eyes again.

"Oh, Paul! She's going to be so happy! She was devastated when she thought you were . . . gone."

A look of regret crossed his face. "I'm a little worried about that. I'm afraid any joy she might feel at the sudden discovery that her . . . *dead* son is alive is going to be quenched by the realization that her *other* son is a traitor."

Something else occurred to Vali, and she leaned toward him, a note of urgency in her voice when she asked, "Paul, that day in Nashville . . . did you say anything to me about Leda . . . something about not trusting anyone but her?"

169

He thought for a moment, then slowly nodded. "Yes. You remember that?"

She felt almost dizzy with the realization that she hadn't simply been delirious, that she *was* recalling actual events. "What did you mean by it?" she pressed him.

Again he hesitated, then shrugged. "I suppose I was thinking about something that Kevin had said on the phone. He told me I had placed myself in danger by mouthing off to Graham as I had, that I should be extremely careful and trust *no one*. I must have felt threatened enough that I was trying to warn you, too, but still give you an anchor—just in case."

"It will be such an incredible shock to Leda," Vali said softly. "But your mother is a wonderfully strong person. She'll be all right."

"I know she will—her and her unshakable faith," he agreed, smiling.

"What are you going to do now?"

"Get us out of this mess just as fast as possible," he said without hesitation. "I've already been putting pressure on Kevin to wrap it up. He had hoped to keep things status quo until they could get some photos of Graham and his contact together. But after our trip to Cedar Point, I started getting really nervous. I knew that incident with the carousel was no accident. And when Jennifer described the man she'd seen . . . . "

He expelled a sharp breath, rubbed the side of his right leg a moment, then went on. "The night your cottage was broken into—you thought I was in Nashville, remember? And I was. With Kevin. He met me there. I told him that, photos or no photos, I was telling you the truth by the weekend. He agreed and promised to take Graham and his buddy into custody by Saturday. Then I got back and found out what had happened at your cottage . . . . "

He shook his head. "When I heard you telling Graham today about the memory flashes, I knew I'd better not wait

170

any longer. Kevin has said all along they wouldn't *let* you remember. I called him from a pay phone this evening and he agreed to wrap it up tomorrow. I had intended to come over to your place in the morning and tell you the truth."

Determination lined his face. "But we're not waiting. I'm going to call Jeff and have him meet us at Mother's tonight. We'll be safe there until Kevin gets Graham and his pal on a plane."

She looked at him blankly. "Jeff?"

He grinned at her. "Jeff Daly. The new man in Mother's life? He's an Agency man. You don't think the CIA would turn an amateur like me loose without back-up, do you?"

"That's terrible! Leda is interested in Jeff—and she thinks he really cares for her!"

"Ah . . . but he does, angel. He does." His smile broadened even more. "Jeff has developed such a fondness for Sandusky's finest that he's giving some serious thought to retiring in the immediate future. Says it's time he was settling down."

Vali slowly shook her head. It was too much to take in all at once. Life had suddenly become something wonderful and yet something awful at the same time. She had never felt so exhausted, so overwhelmed. She closed her eyes, as if by doing so she could somehow wipe out all the ugliness, the pain, and the confusion of the last three years. But then she remembered that her world wasn't ugly or painful or confusing any longer. Because Paul was alive. Paul was back. Beyond all she had asked or dreamed, the Lord had taken care of her. She opened her eyes.

"Vali . . . can you forgive me? For what I've done to you?" He made no move to touch her, but simply pleaded with his eyes. "There seemed to be no other way. I don't suppose I'll ever know what I would have done," he said, "if I'd been conscious and capable of making decisions for myself. It was all taken out of my hands. You'll never know the guilt I

171

felt, when I finally learned what you'd gone through because of me. Yet I know the Lord was in it. And you'll never know how desperately I've prayed for you."

She lifted a hand and gently touched his face, thinking that he no longer looked like David Nathan Keye. This was Paul . . . her Paul.

"Vali . . . do you think you could still love me . . . as I am now? Could we . . . start all over again?"

She studied his face lovingly. "Oh, Paul, we don't have to start all over," she said softly. "I was already falling in love with David Nathan Keye, but I was afraid to let myself care too much. Afraid even to pray about him . . . about Graham. Somehow I knew the only reason I felt the way I did about . . . David . . . was because he reminded me so much of . . . you. Oh, Paul . . . I never stopped loving you."

His face broke into the tender, adoring smile she had never forgotten, and he reached for her. She smiled and went into his arms as if she'd never been away.

She searched his eyes for the one familiar sign she'd been looking for ever since he'd first begun to tell her his amazing story. There it was, shining out just as brightly as she remembered. The look of love, so long restrained, had finally been set free.

"*Welcome home, Paul,*" she whispered from her heart, just before he reclaimed her love with a long, cherishing kiss.

They shared one blissful moment of sweet reunion before a loud pounding on the door shattered the silence and startled them apart.

18

An hour after Dan and Jennifer—with Sunny in the lead—had come charging into the living room, the two couples sat drinking coffee in the kitchen.

Jennifer, who felt as if she were living through somebody else's fantasy, could not stop staring at David. *Not David,* she giddily reminded herself—*Paul. Paul Alexander. In the flesh.*

She'd been in a state of stupefaction from the moment —*Paul*—had opened the door and welcomed them inside. Having called Vali's cottage and getting no answer, they had guessed where she'd gone. Fearing for her safety, Daniel and Jennifer had stormed into the cottage, prepared to do battle. Instead, they found their attack squelched by the sight of Vali wearing a peculiar little smile and clinging almost possessively to . . . *Paul's* arm.

The singer had immediately reassured Jennifer and Dan that she was all right. Glancing at Paul, she had added mysteriously, "I'm fine. But we have something to tell you. And I think you'd better sit down."

It was a good thing she *had* sat down, Jennifer now mused wryly, because otherwise she probably would have been scaling the walls with excitement. She still felt slightly disoriented. Even though Paul had patiently repeated segments of his explanation more than once, her mind was still groping to understand everything.

Paul now glanced across the kitchen table at her and grinned. "Jennifer, why do I have the feeling you're sitting there trying to decide a fitting punishment for me?"

"Punishment?" She stared at him blankly.

"For misleading you," he explained.

173

Jennifer smiled ruefully at him. "At least now I know why I could never feel totally . . . comfortable about you. It was so frustrating," she said bluntly, "liking you in spite of the fact that I didn't trust you."

"It clears up a couple of things for me, too," Dan added. "That first day we met, when I looked at you with my hands, I got a real surprise."

Paul nodded knowingly. "I got very nervous about that encounter. I had a hunch you might realize something wasn't quite right about my face."

"That's right, Daniel!" Jennifer blurted out. "I remember— you were surprised when I told you he was probably in his thirties. You thought he was younger."

"Thirty-two, as a matter of fact," Paul inserted with a grin.

"There's scar tissue around your hairline, isn't there?" Daniel asked. "From the surgeries?"

Paul's smile was a little forced. "Yes. I have a whole new face, Daniel. Not perfect—but new." He paused. "You said a couple of things. What else?"

"Your music."

Paul looked at him with a puzzled frown. "What was it? I worked for months on changing my style, even my notation."

"It was just a small thing," Dan explained. "You used to have a special little flourish when you modulated between keys that I'd never heard anyone but Paul Alexander use. I don't imagine it's easy for a musician to completely shake that kind of thing."

"Apparently not, since I wasn't even aware I was doing it," Paul replied with a light laugh.

"What *I* want to know," Jennifer said, "is how you managed to . . . come back to life . . . and back into *Vali's* life as a musician."

Paul shrugged. "That wasn't too difficult, actually. I was

174

settled into a California condo for a few months, wrote some songs, waited for the Agency to use their contacts—and before long, I was on records again. It wasn't that difficult to establish a reputation on the Coast as a composer and an accompanist. From there, it was just a matter of getting a meeting with Vali's agent and a couple of producers."

"Where were you," Dan asked suddenly, "during your recovery and while they were getting you ready for your . . . re-entry?"

"Different places," Paul said. "I was in a private—*very* private—clinic in Canada for the first year. Some of the later surgeries were done in Oregon. Later I was moved from one safe house to another until they settled me on the Coast."

Dan was quiet for only a moment before something else occurred to him. "The day you went to Nashville—" he began, leaning forward on his chair "—the same day Vali's cottage was broken into . . . do you remember the talk we had that morning?"

"Yes, I think so. Why?"

"You went to a lot of trouble to fill me in on Vali's background and your own concern about her and Graham. At the time, I didn't understand why you were confiding so much personal information to someone you barely knew." He paused. "You were trying to put me on alert, weren't you? About Vali?"

Paul smiled at his perception. "Exactly. You see, I've had this . . . undercurrent of anxiety all along that, if something should happen to me, there was no one to even suspect that Vali was in danger." He paused to study Dan's face, then continued. "I judged you to be a man who wouldn't be easily deceived, Daniel. And, I sensed you were also a man who'd be willing to involve yourself in another's needs. It was my own somewhat feeble way of trying to provide a little extra insurance for Vali."

When the complete story had been told, the four of them

175

sat in silence for a long time. Once Daniel shook his head as if still trying to assimilate the tale of intrigue he'd just heard. Jennifer darted an occasional covert glance at Paul—who returned each one with a knowing, slightly apologetic smile. Vali simply sat looking at him as if she couldn't get enough of what he referred to as his "new face."

Daniel finally brought an end to the silence by pushing back his chair and standing. The retriever sleeping beside him also stirred and sat up. "I think I'd better take Sunny outside for a bit since it sounds like the rain's let up," he said. "Want to come with me, Paul?"

"Sure." The composer gave Vali's shoulder a light squeeze as he got to his feet. "When we come back, I'll call Jeff. If he can meet us there right away, we'll drive in to Mother's." He glanced at Dan, then at Jennifer. "Daniel, I think you and Jennifer should come with us. Neither of you is safe either until this is finished."

Jennifer waited, watching Dan's face. When he nodded his agreement, she sighed with relief.

"We probably shouldn't stay out here too long," Dan said as they walked along the shore. Now off her leash, Sunny ran ahead of them, occasionally turning and running back to check on her owner. "I think we're right in the center of the so-called 'calm before the storm.' "

"How can you tell?"

"Sunny, for one thing. She gets extremely hyper when there's an electrical storm nearby." With a smile, he lifted his face, enjoying the misty spray off the wind-driven lake but feeling particularly edgy. "And so do I," he added.

"You're probably right. There're some pretty impressive lightning flashes accompanying that thunder, and they seem to be getting closer."

They walked along in companionable silence until Dan said, "All of this must have been extremely difficult for you.

176

Trying to hide your true identity from everyone—even your own mother. Your fear for Vali . . . not to mention concealing your feelings for her. I frankly don't know how you carried it off so well."

"It was Vali who kept me going. I was afraid that Graham would try to get rid of her to insure her silence. I should have realized that drug manipulation is more his style. I think he was probably pressured into the idea of killing her. Not that he ever really cared about her," he added bitterly.

"Well, she should be all right now," Daniel said reassuringly.

"I hope so. Whatever Graham's been giving her may cause her some problems for a while. At least off and on, until she gets it out of her system."

"I think it would be wise to get her under a specialist's care right away," Dan agreed.

"I'll talk to her about it, but I'm sure she'll agree. I wish . . . " he paused, then went on. "I wish you could have known Vali before this, Daniel. She was just beginning to bloom, just starting to find herself, to know her own worth. Up until then, she seemed to depend on other people—on *me*, at that particular time—for her identity. I was trying to encourage her to be herself, to be the person God had made her to be."

They stopped walking. From the abrupt silence, Dan sensed that the musician had temporarily drifted back to the past. They stood quietly, not minding the light, drizzling rain. It was several moments before Paul spoke again.

"I wish there were a way you could continue counseling her, Daniel. She admires you very much."

"Paul, you can do everything I could do for Vali—and more. You have an unbeatable combination to help her: Your love for the Lord, and your love for her. It'll take a lot of prayer and a lot of patience, but my instincts tell me that any man who could survive what you have during the last three years has a generous supply of both."

177

"Thank you, Daniel," Paul said, gripping his hand and shaking it firmly. "For everything. Especially for caring enough to get involved—and on your honeymoon, yet."

Dan grinned. "I anticipate a lifetime honeymoon. We can spare a little time this week for friends." He turned then and called Sunny. "We'd better get back. I don't think it's a good idea to leave the girls alone too long."

As they turned to walk toward the house, Dan sensed the storm's accelerating approach and felt a sudden, intense need to get back to Jennifer. He quickened his pace, the urgency deep inside him now swelling to an almost overwhelming wave of desperation. Hardly aware of the other man's presence at his side, Dan felt driven with the need to get back to Paul's cottage. He suddenly knew that they had been gone too long.

19

After the men left with Sunny, Vali and Jennifer made sandwiches and fresh coffee.

"That lightning is getting fierce," Jennifer said, glancing nervously out a window. "Do you think we should try to find an oil lamp or some candles—just in case?"

"I think there's a lamp out in the sun room. David says he likes to sit out there at night and . . . . " Vali broke off her words with a shy smile. "I wonder how long it will take before I don't call him 'David' anymore?"

Jennifer reached over and squeezed her hand. "Probably not long at all. But somehow I don't think he's going to mind very much *what* you call him—just as long as you continue to look at him with those stars in your eyes."

"None of this seems real to me yet," Vali said softly. "That he's alive . . . after all this time . . . . " Her expression sobered. "I don't suppose anything could spoil my happiness in having him back again, but I can't stop thinking about Graham—what he's done, what he *tried* to do."

"Vali . . . " Still holding on to her hand, Jennifer searched for the right words. "Try not to think about Graham right now. You've been through so much today. There are a lot of things you'll have to face later. But for tonight—why don't you just . . . be grateful?"

Vali looked at her for a long moment, then said, "You're right. Paul will help me through the rest of it, when it's time."

"I think I'd better try to find that lamp now," Jennifer said, turning to leave the kitchen.

The sun room was dark except for the erratic glare of lightning streaking through the glass-enclosed walls. As Jennifer entered, a jolt of apprehension shook her. The jalousie door was standing open. Keeping her eyes on the door, she fumbled with one hand for the light switch on the wall.

She heard the step behind her a second too late. Trying to turn, she felt a painful wrench in her shoulder as someone grabbed her arm and pinned it hard behind her back. At the same time, a rough hand covered her mouth, cutting off her scream.

Her eyes boggled, and her mind went into a spin. With a pounding heart, she realized there were *two* people in the room. One was behind her, holding her in a relentless grip; the other, only inches away from her, now stepped out from the shadows.

Graham! A sudden bolt of lightning illuminated him in an eerie, spectral glow. He stood unmoving, his cold gray eyes appraising her with an impassive, clinical stare. As usual, he wore a precisely tailored gray suit that was incongruous with his surroundings. Another blast of fear swept through Jennifer. There was something terrifying about the sight of Graham standing there like an authoritative, implacable businessman watching her squirm under his gaze.

In her struggle to break away, she twisted her head enough to catch a glimpse of the burly man holding her. The sight of his smooth-domed head and flat, sinister features made her legs threaten to buckle.

"You won't need the light, Mrs. Kaine." Graham's frigid, emotionless voice broke the silence.

Panic surged through Jennifer and made her react. Kicking backward and twisting violently, she caught the man behind her off guard. He loosened his grip just enough for her to break free.

But there was nowhere to run. Graham stood motionless in front of her. The other man was poised, ready to jump at her again. She felt like a trapped animal.

Graham raised a restraining hand. With one long, dispassionate look, he sighed, then spoke. "You've made all this far more difficult than it should have been, I'm afraid. If you and your meddling husband had minded your own business from the beginning, there would have been no need for anyone to get hurt."

A chorus of zigzagging lightning flashes bathed him in an incandescent parade of light and shadows. Jennifer's heart hammered once, then seemed to stop when her gaze met the unfathomable, distant stare of the scientist.

This man doesn't hate me, she thought suddenly, stunned by the unexpected insight. *He doesn't feel anything. He's empty . . . he has an empty soul . . . .* At that moment, she knew with a sickening flash of certainty that Graham Alexander was far more dangerous than any of them had suspected. He simply didn't care. The word *sociopath* darted through her mind, and she cringed inwardly at the terrifying suggestion.

"What are you going to do?" she choked out.

He shrugged without answering. He blinked once, started to speak, then glanced beyond Jennifer's shoulder when he heard Vali's voice coming from the direction of the kitchen.

In desperation, Jennifer screamed out a warning. "Vali . . . get out! Get out of the house!"

"Shut up, you little fool!" The scientist snarled and moved toward her, his hand raised. At the same time, the other man pulled a handgun from the pocket of his black raincoat and yanked her tightly against him with one strong, beefy arm.

When Vali appeared in the doorway, Jennifer screamed at her again, but Graham had already moved to the door. He grabbed Vali, dragging her roughly into the sun room and pushing her toward Jennifer. He then stood scowling at both of them.

The other man released Jennifer from his grasp, but

remained inches away from her.

"You—" he waved the gun at Jennifer "—get over there by the wall. You, too," he ordered Vali, turning the gun on her.

They're going to kill us . . . they're going to shoot us, and then they'll wait in here for Daniel and Paul . . . and they'll kill them, too . . . they'll never have a chance. Jennifer began to pray silently, knowing with sick assurance she was only moments away from death.

The man with the gun grunted a menacing obscenity when she hesitated, then shoved her so hard she fell against the glass wall with a thud. Dazed, she clutched at the glass with both hands to steady herself, then turned to see about Vali.

The singer was facing Graham. Her usually gentle, uncertain gaze was turned on him in incredulous anger.

"How can you do this?" Vali's voice shook violently. "What kind of a monster are you? First you try to kill own brother, then—"

Graham's cold eyes suddenly narrowed. "What exactly are you talking about, Vali?"

Her entire body was now trembling. "*Stop* it! Don't you dare to stand there and patronize me, you insane—"

He closed the distance between himself and Vali in two steps. For the first time, Jennifer saw a glint of feeling in his expression. It was rage.

"Spare me your emotional babbling," he snapped. "I asked you a question. What about Paul?"

Vali lifted her face and glared defiantly into his eyes. "The airplane crash, Graham—that's what I mean," she spat out.

His anger seemed to flare once more, then ebb. In its place fell an icy mask of contempt. "Poor Vali," he finally said in a tone malevolently quiet. "You really should have continued your medication, dear. In your particular case, memory is a

182

definite liability." He sighed, then raised a hand to lightly trace the contour of the singer's lovely, stricken face. Jennifer saw Vali's eyes spark with a mixture of terror and revulsion.

"Such a waste, really," Graham continued. "I'd grown rather fond of you, you know. I even argued quite a strong case for your survival." He paused, staring at her for a moment. Then something seemed to snap shut in his eyes, and he smiled thinly. "Ah, well—you've been a most enlightening experiment, at least. It hasn't been a total loss."

"That's all I've ever been to you, Graham? An experiment?"

"Not entirely," he replied. "There was the matter of making sure you didn't know too much."

"About what you did to Paul."

"Mm. Unfortunately, you do seem to be having . . . memory seizures. Just out of curiosity, dear, what *do* you remember? Or perhaps I should ask you how much you knew to begin with? What exactly did my flag-waving brother tell you?"

"Paul told me everything," she admitted quietly.

"Ah. I was afraid of that. That's why I had to start you on the medication right away. I saved your life, you know," he said suddenly, his eyes widening as if the fact surprised him. "My partners were all for terminating you immediately, but I convinced them that your death coming so soon after your fiance's might be a bit too . . . coincidental for some people. It seemed far more expedient—at that point—to simply keep you under observation."

"And now?" Vali's question was little more than a tremulous whisper.

"Now?" He fingered the collar of his white shirt as he stared at her. "I'm afraid you're no longer useful, dear. In fact, you've become rather a problem."

"So you're going to kill me." She uttered the words flatly, with no real evidence of fear. "Let Jennifer go, Graham. You don't even know her. Or Daniel. You can't possibly have any reason to hurt them."

"You've only yourself to blame for whatever happens to the Kaines, Vali," he said reprovingly. "Had you not gone running to the blind man with your foolishness, they could simply have returned home in blissful ignorance. Now . . ." He let his voice drop off meaningfully.

"Graham, don't . . . please."

He ignored her, glancing at the man with the gun. "Get this over with. I'll go to the front and watch for the other two. Be ready to take care of them when they come in the front door. We need to get out of here."

"*No!*" Vali lunged at him. "You nearly killed him once! You won't hurt him again!" Like a wild animal gone berserk, she hurled herself at the scientist, pounding at him and clawing at his face, screaming and crying while she flailed at him.

Jennifer, too, cried out when the older, heavyset man turned his gun toward Vali.

But it was Graham who stopped him from pulling the trigger. "Wait!" he shouted. Grabbing both of Vali's hands, he held her prisoner. "What are you talking about?"

Jennifer had a sudden sense of what Vali was going to say and tried to stop her, but it was too late.

"*He's alive, Graham!*" Vali flung the words at him in a frenzy, watching his stunned look of bewilderment with apparent satisfaction. "You *failed!* Paul is alive!"

"You really *are* insane, you little fool!" He grabbed her by the shoulders and began to shake her. "Tell me what you mean! If my precious brother is alive, then where is he?"

"He's been right under your nose all along—"

She gasped, pressed a fist to her mouth and stared at him. Obviously, she had just realized that she'd made the entire situation even more dangerous for Paul. She continued to stare at Graham, her face now taut with anxiety.

He tightened his grasp on her shoulders, studying her in ominous silence. "Under my nose?"

Jennifer could almost see his mind working. His eyes glinted with suspicion, his face twisted to a menacing scowl. Suddenly his expression changed, gradually settling into a look of tentative understanding. "Keye," he said quietly.

Vali shook her head furiously "No . . . "

But Graham knew. With a sick presentiment of tragedy, Jennifer saw his hand move to circle Vali's throat. "How long have you known about this?"

Vali's eyes were wild with fear as she shook her head from side to side. "No, you're wrong . . . . "

Graham's face turned even uglier as he brought his other hand to her throat and began to squeeze.

Just then, Jennifer screamed—once in horrified denial, then again in terror at a deafening peal of thunder and a loud, sharp crack outside. She turned to see that a huge old cottonwood tree only a few feet away from the sun room had been struck by lightning. The gale-force wind was driving it on a long descent to the ground.

Vali screamed, and both men jumped as the massive tree pulled free of its roots. Like a slow-motion frame from a silent film, it toppled directly toward them, its heavy-hanging branches dragging a mass of power lines down with it.

Jennifer watched in frozen horror as the entangled wires and tree branches struck the propane gas tanks directly outside the sun room. She saw the regulator on one tank crack as it was hit by a large, heavy branch. A second later, live electric wires sparked across the tank. There was a loud whooshing sound, followed by a blast. Flames shot up, and the glass wall at the end of the room exploded.

The bald man with the gun was closest to the explosion. Rocked by the blast and shards of flying glass, he jumped, only to be hit by a spiraling chunk of plaster from the ceiling. He fell backward, squeezing the trigger of the gun before he hit the floor with an unconscious thud.

Graham whirled around, unknowingly making himself a target of the bullet as he moved. His eyes widened with surprise just before he grabbed his chest and fell, almost knocking Vali over as he went to the floor.

Jennifer ran toward Vali and grabbed her hand. "Let's get out of here!"

With a stunned look, Vali glanced from Jennifer to Graham, lying at her feet. Fingers of fire were already lapping at the garden chairs and tables at the other end of the room. The singer stood, as if molded to the spot, watching the flames snake their way up the shattered wall of the house.

"*Vali! Come on!*" Jennifer tugged at her hand to get her to move.

But Vali pulled free and dropped to her knees beside Graham. "He's still alive!" She stared up at Jennifer through glazed eyes. "I can't leave him here!"

Terrified by the storm and the violence, her emotions rioting, Jennifer glanced from Graham to the other man sprawled a few feet away from the growing flames. Quickly she ran to him, knelt, and tried to get a pulse. It was faint, but there. The room was filling up with thick, heavy smoke. Her eyes watered; her throat burned. "We don't have much time. Let's drag them out of here, get them into the kitchen!"

Coughing and wheezing from the smoke, Jennifer grabbed the older man under the arms and began to drag him awkwardly across the floor.

Vali watched Jennifer only a second, then started to tug at Graham. "I can't see anything!" she cried in a strained voice as she drew him toward the door.

"It won't be as bad in the kitchen!" Jennifer choked out.

But by the time they reached the doorway, the kitchen had also begun filling with smoke. Jennifer pulled the bald man's heavy, unconscious body across the threshold of the room, nearly collapsing from the effort.

Vali appeared the next moment, her eyes red-rimmed and frightened, her face dusted with gray ash. "I've . . . swallowed too much smoke . . . I can't . . . breathe . . . ." She tried to free herself from Graham long enough to catch her breath, but he was a big man and dead weight. She lost her balance, and went down hard on her right foot, screaming with pain as Graham's inert form fell on top of her.

Her own strength going fast, Jennifer somehow managed to push Graham away from Vali. Choking and sobbing weakly, the singer stared up at her through terrified eyes. "Jennifer . . . I think my ankle . . . is broken . . . I can't . . . move it."

"Vali—*try!*" Jennifer pleaded with her. "We have to get out of here!"

"Go . . ." Vali clutched at her chest, then tried to move her foot. The effort made her convulse with agony. "Get Paul! I can't get up . . . ."

"I'll get you out!" Jennifer began to pull at her arms.

"No!" Vali looked at Graham. "I can't . . . leave him."

"He tried to kill you!"

"He meant . . . something to me! And he's Paul's brother! Besides . . . it will take you too long!" She locked her hand around Jennifer's wrist. "Jennifer—if you don't . . . go for help . . . fast . . . neither of us will get out of here! *Go!*"

Frantic with fear and indecision, Jennifer looked wildly from Vali to the unconscious men on the floor. Her human nature could have left both men where they were. But she knew Vali was right. She had to try to get Graham out, and the other man as well.

"Jennifer . . . please . . . go."

She scrambled to her feet and bolted from the kitchen, staying low but moving as fast as she could through the dinette and living room. Her lungs struggled for air; her throat was on fire. Tears poured from her eyes. By the time she reached the front door, she was fighting for every breath. She practically fell out the door and onto the porch. The sight of a power pole toppling over, tearing down tree branches and power lines as it fell into the yard, brought a strangled scream of terror from her as she collapsed.

Dan heard the tearing crunch as lightning hit the power pole and ripped through the trees, immediately followed by Paul's rasp of horror.

He pivoted toward the sound of Paul's voiceless scream and started toward him, but Sunny blocked him with her body. He stumbled, barely catching himself from falling over the retriever. "What—"

He heard a hissing, crackling sound, felt heat. His eyes burned; his throat tightened. He swallowed hard, then ordered Sunny to move. He tugged at her leash, but the retriever refused to budge.

"Sunny—forward!"

The guide dog stood unmoving, her body pressing against his to prevent him taking a step. Suddenly he heard Paul's agonized whisper above the sparking, crackling sounds and the rolling thunder.

"Dan—don't move!" Paul's whispered cry sounded as if he were in agony. "You're surrounded . . . by live electric wires! I'm . . . trapped under a tree. My bad leg is . . . caught." He stopped, then choked out, "Dan—the house . . . the house . . . is on fire!"

Dan stood, paralyzed with helpless rage and fear. He could hear the pounding of his heart even above the roaring din of flames and wind. He had never felt so impotent, so worthless in his life.

Merciful Lord . . . what do I do?

"Dan . . . stay where you are . . . whatever you do . . . don't move." Paul's tortured whisper only reminded him of his helplessness.

188

He felt the warm strength of Sunny's body pressing against the front of his legs, heard her whimper softly, sensing her fear as surely as she must sense his. He felt himself weave. Lightheaded, he pulled in a steadying gulp of air . . . smoke singed his lungs, burned his eyes, his nose. His head reeled, then cleared . . .

"Daniel!"

It was Jennifer!

Weak with relief, he turned in the direction of her voice. "Jennifer . . . where are you? Are you all right?"

Her voice came closer. "Daniel . . . oh, Daniel . . . I can't get to you! You're . . . there are electric wires all around you . . . "

"Stay back!" he warned her.

"Daniel . . . Vali's still inside. She's hurt! And Graham is in there. He's been shot! And I think the other man . . . the bald headed man . . . is dying. Vali told me to get help . . . I came to get you and Paul. Where *is* Paul, Daniel, he has to—"

She stopped, and Dan heard her gasp. "Paul! Daniel, what should I do? Paul is trapped under a tree! And you can't move . . . " Her voice was shrill and thready with mounting panic.

Fighting his own terror, Dan made his voice firm and even. "Jennifer . . . listen to me . . . " He heard her sob.

"*Jennifer!*"

She was silent.

"All right now," he said soothingly. "Just . . . listen to me. Sunny can get me out of here, but you're going to have to help. What I want you to do is tell me, one step at a time, which way to move. All you have to do is make sure I don't step too far one way or the other. Sunny will do the rest." He was surprised to hear how steady his voiced sounded. "Do you understand, honey? You have to help me get out of here fast, so I can help Paul and the others. Okay, kid?"

When he heard her small sound of assent, he took a deep

breath and gripped the retriever's leash firmly. "I'm going to come out of here now, Jennifer. Sunny—forward."

The dog hesitated, then moved. Something cracked. Dan stopped, saying evenly, "Help me, Jennifer. Tell me exactly how many steps I can take."

He winced at the tremor in her voice. She sounded one beat away from hysteria. "Y-you need to move to your left. Only a couple of steps, though."

Dan and the dog stepped left. Twice.

"Now what, Jennifer? Tell me what to do."

"Ah . . . I think you . . . yes, come forward. Just . . . one small step, then move right. Another step. One more, Daniel."

He heard her fighting for control, prayed she'd hold together long enough for him to get free of the wires.

He was perspiring heavily, both from his fear and from the heat of the fire. "Quickly now, Jennifer. Help me."

"Don't move!" Her voice shrilled, then fell. "All right . . . step forward just slightly, then to your left. Very carefully. Just small steps, Daniel . . . be careful . . . yes, . . . all right, now . . . another step forward."

Dan's hand clamped the leash in a death grip as his wife and his dog led him out of the maze of live wires. Finally he felt Jennifer's hand on his.

"You—you're out now, Daniel . . . it's . . . it's all right now." She fell into his arms, sobbing wildly.

Holding her tightly for one brief moment, Dan said, "Shh . . . no time for that now, darlin'. You have to take me to Paul so I can get him out from under that tree."

Fighting for control, she took his hand and led him to Paul. While Jennifer supported his shoulders and tried to comfort him, Dan felt for the tree, rapidly walking the length of it, his hands feeling its contour and size. The trapped man writhed, his face contorted in pain.

"Jennifer, I can do this without you. Run to the nearest

cottage and get someone to call the fire department. Then come right back to me."

She hesitated, then got up and took off running.

Dan bent his knees, swelled his shoulders and began to lift. He stopped once, sensing Paul's voiceless scream of pain, then heaved again, lifting until he heard the composer gasp with relief. Half-stumbling under the burden of weight, he pushed the tree far enough out of the way to help the injured man crawl free.

Jennifer returned almost immediately, just as the heavy clouds tore open and it began to pour sheets of rain. Dan raised his face in surprise when he felt the downpour. He knelt down beside Paul. "I have to go after Vali and the others. Can you hold out a few more minutes, buddy?"

Paul clutched at Dan's shoulder, pleading with him. "Don't let her get burned, Daniel . . . the pain is . . . awful . . . get her out." Then he fell back onto the wet grass.

Dan stood, pulled in a long, ragged breath, and said, "Jennifer, the only way I can do this is if you go with me. You'll have to be my eyes."

Her voice was unsteady but determined when she answered. "Let's go."

After making it clear to Sunny that she was to stay with Paul, Dan groped for Jennifer's hand. Placing it on his forearm, he covered it with a firm grip. "Where are they?"

"In the kitchen. The men are unconscious. Vali hurt her ankle."

"Steady, kid," he cautioned her as they headed toward the house. "When we get to the door, get down on your hands and knees. I'm going to put my hand around your ankle, and we'll crawl through to the kitchen. Don't go too fast—and don't stand up."

Jennifer began to move, guiding Dan toward the front porch, weaving in and out of fallen branches and live wires.

191

Dan could hear crackling and popping all around them. The wind lashed angrily through the trees, and the rain pelted them harder than ever.

They reached the front door, and Jennifer got down on her knees, waiting for Dan to lock his hand around her ankle.

The two of them started to crawl slowly and carefully through the living room. The flames had not yet reached this far, but the smoke was dangerously thick and dark. He heard Jennifer mutter, "It's so hard to see . . . "

Dan felt a moment of alarm. He could handle not being able to see—he was used to it. But what if Jennifer panicked?

"I see her, Daniel!" Jennifer cried out, then choked. She stopped, gagging and coughing so hard she could barely breathe. Dan urged her on, his hand on her foot pushing her forward.

"We're in the kitchen, Daniel. She's just ahead. Vali! Vali! We're coming." Again Jennifer dissolved into broken coughs.

Dan's chest felt as if it would explode from the smoke and his fear, but he kept on crawling, holding firmly to Jennifer's ankle.

"How much farther?" he choked out.

"Not far . . . a foot, maybe two."

"Keep going."

As soon as they reached Vali, Dan checked for a pulse. She was unconscious, but her pulse was strong.

He was swallowing smoke now. The lining in his throat felt raw. "Jennifer, are you all right?"

"Yes . . . " She coughed hard, then again. "I'm okay. But Daniel . . . the fire's . . . moving through the door . . . part of the wall is gone. . . the floor is burning."

"We have to hurry. Can you see the others?"

"Here's Graham . . . " She moved Dan's hand to Graham's

192

chest. "Oh . . . he's been burned, Daniel . . . his leg . . . and one hand. It must be from the floor."

Even in the horror of the moment, Dan couldn't help but think of the terrible irony of what had happened. Graham had been responsible for Paul being badly burned. Now Graham, too, was caught in a fire.

He heard Jennifer gag and gasp for breath. "Jennifer . . . what about the other guy? Where is he?"

Her silence panicked him. "Jennifer?"

"I . . . I'm . . . all right . . . here's the other man."

Quickly, Dan lowered his head to the man's chest. His heartbeat was weak but audible.

"Is he alive?"

"Barely. Jennifer—do you think you can drag Vali out if I take Graham? We'll have to come back for the other one."

"Yes . . . I think so."

"Get a good grip under her arms. I won't be able to hold your ankle, so go slow enough that I don't lose track of you. Can you see anything?"

"Just . . . no, not really . . . it's all smoke . . . Dan—" Her voice suddenly grew shrill.

"It's all right. Here we go, kid . . . you first . . . go on . . . we're all right."

He was acutely aware that their time was limited. In spite of the rain, the blaze was moving and could sweep the house any moment. For once, his handicap was more of an advantage than a burden. He didn't need to see in order to crawl, and he didn't have to see to pull a limp body along behind him. All he had to do was stay with Jennifer. And pray.

. . . When you pass through the waters, I will be with you; and through the rivers, they will not overflow you. When you walk through the fire, you will not be scorched, nor will the flame burn you . . .

The enormous lung capacity he'd developed over years of training to be an Olympic swimmer was serving him well. He could hold his breath for an incredibly long time, and he used that ability now to keep from being overcome by smoke.

. . . He shall cover thee with His feathers, and under His wings shalt thou trust . . .

He felt a little more secure when he touched the softness of the living room carpet. Suddenly he heard Jennifer begin to wheeze. She stopped moving.

"Jennifer?"

She didn't answer.

His eyes felt as though they were on fire, his skin felt scorched. "Jennifer—don't give up now. We're almost out. Don't give up, honey."

He felt a light movement, heard her gasp. Then they began to move again, slower, much slower now. She coughed again, then choked and gagged. But she kept going. His own lungs felt as if they were about to explode.

He heard a loud whoosh behind them and knew the fire was sweeping the kitchen.

. . . The Lord will guard your going out and your coming in from this time forth and forever . . .

At that moment, he felt a touch of damp night air from the partly opened front door. "Jennifer?"

"Yes—I'm out! Come on . . . Daniel . . . hurry!"

Finally, with Graham firmly in tow, Dan crawled onto the porch. From a distance . . . so far away it seemed to be coming from another world, another time . . . he heard the urgent wail of approaching fire engines. Then voices. Someone helped them off the porch. He sighed with weak relief when he felt the wet grass under his hands.

. . . the fire had not harmed their bodies, nor was a hair of their heads singed . . .

Dan heard a fire truck screech to a halt, its siren still wailing loudly. He raised one limp hand to hail someone, heard the wet smacking sound of a fireman's rain slicker beside him. He was able to choke out, "Another man . . . inside . . . "

He felt Jennifer's arms go around him, felt her heavy, wet hair falling over his face. "Daniel . . . oh, Daniel . . . are you all right?"

"I don't know, kid. Do I look all right?" He smiled foolishly.

"You look beautiful," she sobbed. "Your face is black, and your eyes are all red, and your clothes are ruined. But you look beautiful, Daniel . . . " She hugged him to her, smothering his ash-covered face with kisses.

"We're quite a team, kid . . . "

"We're a *great* team, Daniel . . . " She sniffed, then hugged him even tighter.

"One thing, though, darlin' . . . "

"Yes, Daniel?" She cried harder.

"Now that I've seen . . . your idea of a honeymoon . . . would you mind very much . . . if I . . . plan our vacations?"

Epilogue

November

"I still can't believe we're here, Daniel. This has to be one of the most exciting things that's ever happened to me!"

"Thanks," Daniel said dryly, smiling as the enthusiasm in her voice spilled over like a runaway waterfall. "Where are our seats?"

"Orchestra section," Jennifer said distractedly, her head swiveling back and forth to watch the crowd pouring into The Performing Arts Center.

"Mm. First class. Do you see Leda anywhere?"

"No. I can't see much of anything from here."

A red-haired man wearing a sports coat and sweater vest walked up to them and smiled. "Mr. and Mrs. Kaine? I'm Grandy Hayden—Paul's manager. He asked me to meet you." He shook hands with both Dan and Jennifer, glancing with interest at Sunny, who stood patiently at Dan's side on her leash.

"Your seats are down front. Paul's mother is already there. I'll take you to her, if you like."

He stepped in front of them and started walking. "Have you been at TPAC before?"

"No, we haven't," Dan replied. "We've been in Nashville, but this is our first time at the Center."

"Looks like most of Nashville is here tonight," Hayden said, glancing around. "I think we're going to have people hanging from the ceiling before long." He stopped to let someone pass, then went on. "Paul says the two of you are providing the music for the wedding tomorrow."

Jennifer nodded energetically, trying to ignore the

196

butterflies in her stomach.

The concert hall was enormous, and already every inch of available space, both downstairs and in the tiered balcony, was packed.

As they neared the front, Jennifer spotted Leda, who stood when she saw them and waved. She warmly embraced both of them when they reached their seats, and Jeff Daly, at her side, stood and shook hands. Then Leda introduced Vali's Aunt Mary, who was sitting on the other side of Jeff. Grandy Hayden waited until they were settled in their seats, with Dan and Sunny on the aisle, then left to go backstage.

Still holding onto Jennifer's hand as they sat down, Leda exclaimed, "I think I'm more excited than the kids tonight! Isn't this an event, though? The two of them together on a stage again for the first time in over three years?" She glanced at Dan, then back at Jennifer. "So—are you ready for this big weekend? I'm already exhausted! And Vali—" She rolled her eyes heavenward. "I don't think that child has slept for a week! I told her she's going to collapse before the wedding tomorrow if she doesn't get some rest, but she doesn't hear me—she's too busy!"

Dan grinned at her strident chatter and asked, "How's Paul doing? Is he nervous?"

Leda arched one dark brow in amusement. "About the concert? No. He doesn't get too hyper about performing. But the wedding?" She shook her head and threw up both hands. "He's no longer coherent."

As if by mutual consent, no one mentioned the forthcoming trial. Jennifer knew it had to have been a shattering experience for Leda to have one son returned to her while losing the other son to an extended prison sentence. According to recent newspaper accounts, both Graham and his cohort would be behind bars for years once they recovered from their injuries and were able to stand trial.

With a meaningful glance at Jeff Daly, Jennifer lowered her voice to a conspiratorial whisper and asked, "Is it possible there's going to be another wedding in the near future, Leda?"

"It's under discussion," she answered slyly. "But I think we'll elope. I'd never muster the energy to survive two big—"

The sudden dimming of the lights, once, then again, followed by a crashing, reverberating stream of synthesized chords made her stop and turn toward the stage.

Jennifer clutched Dan's hand in almost unbearable anticipation as the music continued to echo from a darkened stage. The waiting crowd began to cheer, already recognizing the unique sound of Paul Alexander's music.

A spotlight isolated Grandy Hayden as he hurried onstage, and the music ebbed to a soft backdrop when he started to speak. He grinned and waited to make himself heard.

"I won't draw this out—" the crowd applauded "—you've waited long enough. There's nothing I could tell you that you probably don't already know anyway. By now you've heard their story . . . you know where they've been and what they've gone through." His expression sobered and he paused a beat before going on. "Three years ago, you thought you'd told them goodbye." His smile returned. "Now, say hello . . . to Vali Tremayne and Paul Alexander . . . by the grace of God—together again!"

He made a sweeping gesture with one hand, backing off the stage as the lights went up and the music thundered and the crowd hit their feet in unison, exploding into a deafening roar of cheering applause.

"Tell me *everything*," Daniel said in a voice loud enough to be heard above the crowd and the music as he and Jennifer scrambled to their feet along with everyone else in the auditorium.

198

"There's Paul! Oh—Daniel—there he is!" Jennifer cried, clutching eagerly at Dan's arm. "He's at his synth! Oh, my goodness . . . he looks so different! He's gained weight . . . and his hair is darker again . . . it still has lots of silver, though . . . and he still has a beard . . . he looks *wonderful!* He looks *happy!* And he's still chewing gum, bless his heart!"

The din in the hall broke the pain barrier as Paul and his group moved into the hit contemporary Christian song associated with Vali throughout her meteoric career. She half-walked, half-ran onto the stage, even lovelier than Jennifer remembered in pink Victorian lace, her magnificent hair blazing about her head. She faced the people once, opening her arms wide in welcome, then crossed to Paul and took him by the hand.

The two of them came center-front, their faces beaming with love for the crowd and for each other. Vali frequently had to wipe the tears from her eyes. Once she was overcome and pressed her head against Paul's shoulder for a moment until she regained her composure.

Leda was crying openly. It seemed to Jennifer that everyone in the hall was crying, and she was no exception. Daniel, too, was dabbing at his eyes with his handkerchief.

It took almost ten minutes before the crowd settled down, and even then Paul had to force it. Taking a microphone, his eyes twinkled with fun as he whispered, "For those of you who were expecting David Nathan Keye, I apologize for the last minute switch."

After their laughter subsided, he grinned at them and asked, "Well—you want to stand here and cry all night, brethren, or do you want some music?"

Their uproar made it clear they wanted music. And they got music—a wide variety. They had the well-loved and familiar numbers Vali and Paul had made popular years before—the golden oldies, as Paul referred to them. They had a wealth of new numbers Paul had turned out since moving back to Nashville . . . they had hand-clapping, joy-sounding praise songs . . . they had slow, melodic melodies like *Vali's Song* . . . they had gospel songs and hymns and Scripture-singing songs . . . years of treasured Christian music poured out as a love offering to the Lord in the presence of the people of the Lord.

"Vali seems so much more confident," Jennifer remarked to Dan once, noting the pleased smile her words brought to his face. "She's absolutely . . . awesome up there!"

"We're in the presence of greatness, kid," he said, meaning it.

"They're so *good* together, Daniel."

"Like us," he said with a sage nod.

"Like us," she repeated, checking his expression for any hint of levity but finding none.

Returning her attention to the stage, she saw Paul grab a microphone and drape his other arm around Vali. He looked exhausted but happy as he began to address the crowd.

"We really have to quit some time tonight, people," he said. He met the chorus of protests from the audience with an upraised hand and a grin. "Wait . . . wait a minute . . . just in case there's anyone out there who doesn't know this by now, I have something to tell you."

He brought the mike a little closer to his mouth and leaned forward to the audience, his eyes sparkling with infectious mischief. His teasing grin broke into a broad smile of unrestrained joy as he whispered dramatically, "We're . . . getting . . . married . . . tomorrow."

He turned to a prettily blushing Vali and kissed her soundly with loud and energetic audience approval.

Paul waited until the din subsided, then spoke again into the microphone, slowly and distinctly so his whisper-voice could be understood.

"Tonight is a special time of reunion for Vali and me. Our being together again is a miracle for which we'll never cease to thank God. We're grateful beyond words to be able to stand up here together and look out and see the people we love. Among those people are two very special friends the Lord brought into our lives at a time when we needed them most."

Paul smiled out at them and continued. "Most of you have probably heard of one member of this marvelous duo. A few months ago, a musical drama by the title of *Daybreak* swept the Christian community. Not only has the musical itself changed numerous lives, but the title song has become an anthem of hope for Christians throughout the country. It will be a part of our wedding service tomorrow, but we wanted to share it with you tonight. *Daybreak* was written by a wonderful man named Daniel Kaine, who has a beautiful wife named Jennifer. We'd like you to meet both of them . . . right now."

The next thing Jennifer knew, Paul had bolted from the stage, slowed very little by his stiff leg, and was headed toward her and Daniel. The crowd broke into pleased applause as he embraced them, then linked arms with both of them and coaxed them up to the stage with him, where they were welcomed by a misty-eyed Vali, who gave each of them—including Sunny—a fervent hug.

A moment later, after Paul had led Dan to the grand piano and returned to his synthesizer, a hush fell over the entire auditorium. Dan hesitated only a moment before sounding the opening chords of *Daybreak*. Paul waited a few measures, then added the electronic equivalent of a full orchestra, and the two of them began to offer a sacrifice of praise that Jennifer felt sure had the angels in heaven singing with them.

Finally she and Vali added their voices to the music and joined Dan at the piano.

There was neither a dry eye in the auditorium nor a person remaining in their seat as the four of them repeated the *Daybreak* finale again and again, building its volume as they built its emotion, giving their voices, their hearts, and their spirits over to the music that God had used time after time, first for Daniel . . . and now for others.

Standing behind her husband, watching the mastery and the consummate skill of his hands at the keyboard, feeling the power in his massive shoulders as he played and the power in his spirit as he gave, Jennifer had a sudden flash of insight that shook her to the very core of her being.

She looked up from Daniel and out into the mass of people whose voices were raised in one thundering hymn of communal praise and saw, not a sea of strangers, but a family of loved ones. In that moment, she thought she might have caught a glimpse of what their Lord had wanted for His children from the beginning of creation . . . a oneness, a unity of heart and spirit and purpose with the power to transcend individual needs, bridge nations, unite governments, and join worlds as a body fitted together and secured in place by the love of Jesus Christ.

As if he could read her thoughts, Dan gave up the piano to rise and join his wife and friends. Paul came to join them, and the four of them linked hands and walked to the front of the stage, basking in the unity and the love filling the hall.

As the closing notes sounded, faded and echoed across the immense, overflowing auditorium, Jennifer glanced from Vali to Paul, then to the audience, and finally to her husband.

"What are you thinking, Daniel?" she asked, close to his ear in order to be heard.

He hugged her tightly and gave her a smile that went straight to her heart. "I was thinking," he said quietly, "about how much the Father must enjoy these family reunions."

OTHER ACCENT BOOKS BY B.J. HOFF:

Mists of Danger

"Daybreak Mystery" Series:
   Storm at Daybreak
   The Domino Image